THE INNOCENT'S SINFUL CRAVING

BY

SARA CRAVEN

MILLS & BOON

2016

First published in Great Britain 2015
By Mills & Boon, an imprint of HarperCollins*Publishers*
1 London Bridge Street, London, SE1 9GF

Large Print edition 2016

ISBN: 978-0-263-26175-2

Our policy is to use papers that are natural, renewable and recyclable products and made from wood grown in sustainable forests. The logging and manufacturing processes conform to the legal environmental regulations of the country of origin.

Printed and bound in Great Britain
by CPI Antony Rowe, Chippenham, Wiltshire

For Leo, stern critic and amazing support.

CHAPTER ONE

AT THE TOP of the hill, she stopped the car on the verge and got out, stretching gratefully after the drive from London.

The house lay below her in its secluded green valley, a sprawl of stones like some ancient dragon sleeping in the sunlight.

Dana drew a long, satisfied breath, her taut mouth relaxing into a smile of pure pleasure.

'I've come back,' she whispered. 'And this time I'm going to stay. Nothing—and no one—is going to drive me away again. You're going to be mine. Do you hear me?'

And after one final, lingering look, she returned to the car and drove down the hill towards Mannion.

It would not—could not be the same. For one thing, there would be no Serafina Latimer with her kindness and smiling grace that could so suddenly change to severity. She was back in her beloved Italy, and Aunt Joss, of course, had gone with her.

But I've changed too, she thought.

She was a long way from the confused seventeen-year-old who'd left here seven years earlier, physically, emotionally and—yes, she supposed, even financially.

No longer the housekeeper's niece, there on sufferance, for ever on the outside looking in, but a successful and well-paid negotiator with a top London estate agency.

And the past years of fighting her way up the ladder, reinventing herself into a force to be reckoned with, had taught her a lot.

I've helped a lot of people make their dream come true, she thought. Now, it's my turn.

Except that Mannion wasn't simply a dream. It was her birthright, whatever the law might say. There was such a thing as natural justice, and she would lay hold to it, no matter what means she had to employ. Or what the consequences might be.

She'd decided that a long time ago, and the passage of time had only deepened her resolve.

She drove through the tall wrought-iron gates

and up the long drive through the sweeping lawns and formal gardens to the house. There were already cars parked on either side of the main entrance and she slotted her Peugeot into the nearest available space.

Climbing out, she stood for a moment, scanning the other vehicles, steadying the sudden flurry of her breathing, and smoothing any creases from her khaki linen skirt before collecting her weekend case from the boot.

As she turned she saw that the heavily studded front door had opened and a plump woman in a neat dark dress was waiting there.

'Miss Grantham?' Her voice was quietly civil. 'I'm Janet Harris. Let me take your case and show you to your room.'

I probably know the way better than you do, Dana thought, amused, as she followed the housekeeper. How many times have I trotted round after Aunt Joss, making sure everything was ready for arriving guests? Sometimes even being allowed to put the flowers in the bedrooms.

I wonder if anyone's done that for me?

The answer to that, she soon discovered was 'no', along with the fact that she'd been allocated the smallest of the guest rooms in the remotest part of the house, looking over the shrubbery to the slope of the valley where the summer house still stood.

The one thing she had no wish to see. That she'd hoped would no longer exist, although the memories it evoked were still potent. Bitterly and disturbingly so.

However the choice of view was probably not deliberate, she thought, turning from the window. Unlike the selection of the room with its faded decor and elderly carpet, seemingly intended to put her firmly in her place.

That's fine, she thought. When the game's over, let's see who's won.

'The bathroom is just down the corridor, Miss Grantham.' Mrs Harris sounded almost apologetic. 'But you'll have it to yourself. If there's anything else you need, please let me know.' She paused. 'Miss Latimer asked me to say there is tea in the drawing room.'

How very formal, Dana thought with faint amusement as the housekeeper withdrew. And how very unlike Nicola. But perhaps she was finding it was rough going being a hostess.

She hadn't much to unpack apart from her dresses for this evening and tomorrow night's party which she hung in a wardrobe as narrow as the single bed.

The bathroom was basic but well supplied with towels, a tub with a hand shower and a full-length mirror.

So, having combed her hair, replenished her lipstick and freshened her scent, Dana inspected herself with the same critical intensity she expected to encounter downstairs.

Her light brown hair, well-cut and highlighted so that it glowed with auburn lights, hung, smooth and shining, to her shoulders, and the subtle use of cosmetics had emphasised the green of her hazel eyes and lengthened her curling lashes.

Her body, rounded in all the right places, was slim and toned thanks to the exercise and dance classes she attended with zealous regularity. Not cheap, but the end would justify the means.

And Nicola's unstudied greeting of ten days ago had also been reassuring. 'Dana, it's wonderful to see you again. And you look amazing.'

A total exaggeration, but gratifying just the

same, she thought as she started on her way downstairs.

Now that she had time to look around her, she realised it wasn't only her bedroom that needed refurbishment. The whole house looked tired and shabby and it was all too evident that the high standards of cleanliness observed in Aunt Joss's day had slipped badly.

Surfaces no longer glowed as they once had. There was no beguiling mixture of lavender and beeswax in the air, and in places there were even cobwebs.

It all looked—unloved, but perhaps that was what happened when the mistress of the house was no longer in residence.

Not that Serafina Latimer had enjoyed much choice in the matter. Once she'd decided to avoid Inheritance Tax by gifting Mannion to Nicola's older brother Adam, she was allowed only casual and infrequent visits to her former home in the seven-year period it took for the gift to become legal and Adam to become Mannion's full owner.

Aunt Joss had explained it all to Dana in some detail, brushing aside all attempts at questions or protests, before adding with chill emphasis,

'So, once and for all, let that be an end to this nonsense.'

Yet, how could it be, when Dana knew, as surely as the sun rose in the east, that she had been passed over?

Her rightful inheritance given away like some free bar of soap?

Knew too that her aunt was wrong, and the fight was far from over.

Poor Mannion, she thought, as she reached the foot of the stairs. But when you're mine, you won't be passed from hand to hand again.

And this time there'll be no one around to stop me.

There was none of the expected buzz of conversation as she approached the dining room, and she found herself hesitating briefly before entering.

For a moment, as she took in the old-fashioned chintzes that covered the deep sofas and armchairs, and saw the long brocade curtains moving gently in the faint breeze from the open French windows, she felt as if she'd stepped back in time.

Then, in the same instant, she realised that she'd totally misread the housekeeper's message, because it was quite another Miss Latimer waiting for her behind the tea table. A much older version, her plump girth squeezed into unbecoming floral silk, her bleached hair like a metal helmet, her lips pursed.

Nicola's Aunt Mimi, she thought with a silent groan. Oh, God, I should have known.

'Well, Dana.' She was motioned to a chair by a beringed hand. 'This is a surprise.' Mimi Latimer's tone suggested it was more of an unpleasant shock. 'I didn't realise that you and Nicola were still in touch, let alone so close.'

Dana smiled, unfazed. 'Good afternoon, Miss Latimer. No, sad to say, we probably haven't seen so much of each other lately.' Seven years to be precise. 'But I'm sure you remember that we were at school together.'

'Yes,' Mimi Latimer said with a touch of grimness as she poured straw-coloured Earl Grey into a fragile cup and held it out to Dana. 'I certainly hadn't forgotten that. Or that your scholastic career came to a sudden end. A poor reward for all Serafina's kindness to you.'

'Perhaps we both felt she'd been quite kind enough,' Dana returned coolly. 'And that it was time I stood on my own feet.' Besides, it was recognition as her granddaughter I wanted—not her charity.

'I don't think anyone would argue over that,' Miss Latimer said with a sniff, proffering a plate of sandwiches smaller than a child's finger.

That, and a Madeira cake, comprised the entire spread, Dana realised, remembering coming back for the school holidays to find the table laden not just with sandwiches but scones and cream, or buttered crumpets, depending on the season, to be followed with a rich chocolate cake and a Victoria sponge oozing strawberry jam. And Serafina presiding over these delights, gently questioning Nicola and herself on how the term had gone.

'And your family. Are they well?'

Memories scattered under Mimi Latimer's acidly pointed question.

'All fine, thank you.' At least on the rare occasions when I have news.

But the older woman had not finished. 'And your mother? Still living in Spain?'

'Yes,' Dana confirmed evenly. 'She is.'

'And you seem to be doing well too. Trying to sell Nicola and Eddie an expensive flat, I gather.'

'I've shown them a very beautiful flat,' Dana corrected, helping herself to an egg and cress sandwich and making it stretch to two bites. 'Well within the price guidelines she and her fiancé had established, and which they both seemed to like.'

'How strange it should be you showing them round.'

'I prefer to call it serendipity,' Dana said lightly. 'A happy discovery by accident.' Apart from the wheeling, dealing and sheer manipulation it took to ensure I conducted that particular viewing.

She took a reluctant sip of cooling tea. 'Where is Nicola, by the way?'

'Taking Eddie and his parents to see the village church.' Miss Latimer's mouth tightened sourly. 'She's decided she wants to be married there. Quite ridiculous when London would be so much more convenient for everyone.

'But she's managed to persuade Eddie that they should have a quiet country wedding with just family, close friends and local people. As this weekend's gathering was supposed to be,' she added pointedly.

'Heaven only knows what the Marchwoods will think,' she went on peevishly. 'I've tried to talk some sense into the child, but, for some reason, that cousin of Serafina's, the Belisandro man, has taken her side.' She sniffed again. 'Of course, he's always spoiled Nicola, encouraging her to have her own way. I'm only surprised he isn't marrying her himself.'

Dana felt her heartbeat stumble and her throat tighten. She forced down another mouthful of Earl Grey.

When she spoke, her voice was remarkably steady. 'Zac Belisandro hardly seems the marrying kind.'

Besides being safely on the other side of the world. Although it seemed that had not stopped him again pulling strings in the Latimer affairs.

'Well, I dare say his father will have something to say about that before he's much older,' Miss Latimer opined snappishly. 'Not that it's any concern of mine,' she added hastily. 'Or yours for that matter.'

Dana managed a serene smile. 'You're quite right. Gossip can be so damaging.'

The silence that followed seemed to be waiting for her to ask, 'And where is Adam?'

But all hell would freeze over before she said any such thing. Especially to Mimi Latimer.

Anyway, I shall see him soon enough, she thought, allowing her mind to dwell pleasurably on his windblown blond hair and almost boyish good looks, enhanced by the laughter lines at the corners of his blue eyes and the mouth that seemed always ready to smile.

A man that any woman would want, even without the riches he was bringing with him, and she knew it. Had reminded herself over and over again that it justified the course of action she was set upon.

Even so, she was suddenly struggling to hold on to that inner picture. To prevent it being superseded by another image, as disturbing as it was unwelcome. By another face, olive-skinned and saturnine, the features strongly marked, the eyes as dark and impenetrable as a starless winter night.

She put her cup with what remained of the tea carefully back on the table. 'This has been most enjoyable, but, if you'll excuse me, I need to stretch my legs after the drive.'

And, with another smile, she walked across the room and out through the French windows on to the terrace. Where she paused, staring at the lawns below as if in rapt admiration of its billiard table smoothness.

In reality, and in spite of herself, she was listening to her brain frantically re-echoing the name—*Zac Belisandro.*

His father's only son and heir to the vast Belisandro International empire. Currently running its holdings in Australia and the Far East with an aplomb and success that was becoming legendary.

'The man who makes Midas look like a beginner' had been a headline in the business pages of a popular daily.

And to Dana—the man who'd caused her to be sent away from Mannion seven years ago. Her enemy, who would still want her barred now, if he wasn't thousands of miles away.

Don't think of him, she told herself fiercely. Concentrate on Adam. He's the only one who matters and always has been.

But her mind—her memory—would not obey her. Because Zac Belisandro was still there like a shadow in the sunlight.

In spite of the heat, Dana shivered. Just let him stay away, she whispered silently. Don't make me have to see him again. Ever. Or at least until I've got what I want and it's too late for him to interfere and ruin everything a second time.

Until I'm Mrs Adam Latimer and Mannion belongs to me as it always should have done.

Captain Jack Latimer, she thought. Serafina's soldier son and my father. If he hadn't been killed in that ambush in Northern Ireland, my mother's life—and mine—would have been very different. They would have been married, and whatever Serafina thought, she would have had to accept it.

He wouldn't have allowed the girl he loved to be sent away in disgrace.

She walked down the terrace steps and headed across the lawn to the shrubbery. Ever since she'd first come to live at Mannion, it had been her favourite bolthole, a place to hide in when she was missing her mother and wanted to cry in peace. Aunt Joss was kind enough but too busy and often too harassed to devote much time to her.

And taking charge of her young niece was something Dana knew had been thrust upon her, because her sense of duty would not allow the little girl to be fostered during her mother's frequent and often lengthy absences in hospital.

So, a lot of the time, she was lonely. Not the kind of desolation where she knelt on the other side of a locked door listening, frightened, to her mother's harsh weeping.

It was more a sense of bewildered abandonment which remained even when she and her mother were reunited in some new poky flat, while Linda, each time more fragile, more diminished, struggled with yet another dead-end job, and promised the brisk women who visited her in the evenings with their files of paperwork, that this time she would make an effort—make it work for Dana's sake as well as her own.

She paused, fists suddenly clenching at her sides, as she wondered if she, a small child, had been the only one to see it was never going to happen.

And by that time all that filled her heart and mind was Mannion.

'Our home,' Linda had told her over and over

again, murmuring to her at night in the bed they shared. 'Our security. Our future. Taken away because I was only the housekeeper's sister.

'I thought your grandmother would welcome me when I went to her. Be glad that Jack had a child. I thought we could mourn for him together. Instead she sent us both away. I felt my heart break when I lost your father, but she shattered it all over again.

'But she won't beat us, my darling. Mannion was your father's inheritance, so it belongs to us now and one day we'll take it back. Say it, sweetheart. Let me hear the words.'

And obediently, eyes closing, voice fogged with sleep Dana would whisper, 'One day we'll take it back.'

Not that it helped. Because, all too soon, it would begin again—the soft monotonous sobbing from behind the closed bedroom door, interspersed with the periods where Linda sat by the living room window, unspeaking and unmoving as she stared into space.

When Dana would find herself whisked back to Mannion and Aunt Joss, each time finding herself more secure. Feeling a sense of possession growing as the seeds her mother had planted took root.

Mrs Brownlow, one of the brisk ladies who visited her mother, was now calling at Mannion for regular conferences with Aunt Joss.

Sometimes, she caught snatches of their conversation. 'Such a difficult situation...' 'Not the child's fault...' 'Very bright at school, but suffering from these disruptions...'

And over and over again from Aunt Joss: 'This unhealthy obsession...'

One day, Mrs Brownlow had been soothing. 'Linda seems much more upbeat—a real change. We're hoping that this complete break will help get her back on track. She seems to be looking forward to it.'

'Two weeks in Spain?' Aunt Joss had sounded doubtful. 'Without Dana?'

'This first time, yes. To see how she copes. Perhaps we can arrange a joint holiday later on.'

Dana was thankful. Not that she was particularly happy at the village school where the children, confused by her arrivals and departures, treated her as an outsider. But she wasn't altogether sure where Spain was—except that it was almost certainly a long way from Mannion, the only place she really wanted to be.

And where she would fight to stay.

But Linda, it seemed, had given up the fight because, towards the end of the two weeks, Aunt Joss got a letter from her to say she'd got a job in a bar and had decided to stay in Spain for a while.

Her decision had caused uproar among the officials who were handling her case, but Aunt Joss was calm, even philosophical, informing them that it could be for the best and would, at any rate, give Dana the chance of a stable upbringing.

Dana missed her mother but she also felt grateful that the burden of Linda's seemingly endless despair had been lifted from her.

And at least she was living in the place that Linda had wanted for them both, and maybe, in time, Serafina's attitude might soften and she would accept Dana as her granddaughter.

And in another way, Dana's life took a definite change for the better when Nicola arrived to spend the summer at Mannion.

Another orphan of the storm, Dana recalled wryly, her parents acrimoniously divorced, with custody of Nicola and her older brother being awarded to their father. Megan Latimer was now living in the wilds of Colombia with the millionaire boyfriend who had caused the marriage breakdown on an estate rumoured to be like an armed fortress.

'And I'm not allowed to go there,' Nicola had confided as Dana was rather awkwardly showing her the gardens on Serafina's instructions. 'The judge said so, even though I said I liked Esteban.'

She looked woebegone. 'Daddy said we could all go on a sailing holiday, but I didn't want to, because I can't swim very well and I get seasick. So he's just taking Adam, and got Aunt Serafina to say I could come here.'

'It's lovely here,' Dana said. 'You'll like it.' And they exchanged cautious smiles.

In the kitchen garden, Mr Godstow, face ruddy under his faded cap, filled a trug for them with the pods of young, sweet peas, raspberries and gooseberries which they carried off to share in the den Dana had constructed in the shrubbery.

It was a curious form of bonding, but it worked. They'd both been on an emotional see-saw and now, unexpectedly, had found a friend in each other.

Until, of course, Zac Belisandro had engineered their separation.

But I'll have my revenge, she told herself, when Mannion's mine and it's his turn to be barred.

And it would happen. She'd been thwarted once, but since then she'd had a long time to prepare for this second crucial attempt on the glittering prize that had possessed her heart and mind to the exclusion of so much else for so long.

The reunion at the flat viewing had gone like clockwork. Nicola's delight at seeing her again was quite unfeigned, and while Dana might tell herself it was just a means to an end, she knew it wasn't true, and that she was equally thrilled.

'Eddie has to go back to work now,' Nicola said when they joined Dana in the spacious living room after their second, private tour of inspection. 'So why don't we find a bar and have a double celebration?'

'Double?'

'Of course.' Nicola's wide grin was just the same. 'Finding our future home and you, again, at the same time.'

'Two wonderful reasons,' Dana laughed back. 'Let's go.'

'So what happened to you?' Nicola asked as they toasted each other in Prosecco in a local wine bar. 'Why did you suddenly disappear like that—before your final year at school?'

You mean that Zac Belisandro didn't tell you...

Aloud, she said lightly, 'It wasn't really that sudden. I'd already decided against university, so when that London job came up again, I took it.'

'But you went without a word.' There was hurt in Nicola's voice. 'And you never answered any of my letters although your aunt promised she'd send them on.'

Except her first loyalty was to Serafina, not her own disgraced, illegitimate niece, exiled before she caused more trouble.

Dana swallowed. 'Well, I did move around quite a bit. The letters are probably still in the system, trying to track me down.'

'Well, I shan't let you slip away again,' Nicola said resolutely. 'We're having a family get-to-gether down at Mannion the weekend after next to talk wedding plans and you're going to be there. And I won't take no for an answer.'

'I wouldn't dream of it,' Dana said with perfect truth, her mind reeling.

'It will be just like old times,' Nicola went on. 'Jo and Emily are going to be there, as they're my bridesmaids, and they're bringing their blokes.' She paused. 'So, if you've got someone in your life, invite him along.'

Dana took another mouthful of Prosecco. 'There's no one serious. Not at the moment.'

But that would all change—down at Mannion.

Nicola sighed. 'You sound like Adam. As soon as I get to like one of his girlfriends, he's on to the next.' She pulled a face. 'And Zac, the serial monogamist, sets him a bad example.'

'I can imagine.' Dana's mouth felt suddenly stiff. 'Maybe Adam just hasn't met the right woman yet.' Or not at the right time.

Afterwards, she'd been assailed by doubts, telling herself that it couldn't possibly be that simple, half expecting a call from Nicola telling her that the weekend had been cancelled or making some other excuse.

Instead she'd had a call from Eddie offering the full asking price on the flat, and when Nicola phoned a few days later, it was to confirm the invitation and say how much everyone was looking forward to seeing her again.

Including Adam? wondered Dana, but did not dare ask.

Although she would soon find out, she thought now, glancing at her watch. It was time to stop skulking in the grounds and begin her campaign.

She was halfway across the lawn when she realised she was being watched. That a man was standing, silent and unmoving, at the head of the terrace steps.

For one jubilant instant, she thought, *Adam*...

Then her footsteps faltered as she realised her observer was much too tall to be Adam. And much too dark.

Dark as midnight. Dark as a bad dream.

Only she wasn't dreaming. Not this time. She was looking at Zac Belisandro—not on the other side of the world but, by some ill chance, right here.

Waiting for her.

CHAPTER TWO

No!

The word was in her throat like a silent scream. Because it couldn't be true. Yet the wild, unruly thud of her terrified heart told her there was no room for doubt.

She couldn't run. There was nowhere to go and, anyway, she wouldn't give him the satisfaction of putting her to flight.

But he wouldn't be able to get rid of her this time. Serafina was no longer around to sit in judgement on a young girl who'd offended her code of conduct.

This time, she was Nicola's guest. One of the gang. And Nicola would laugh to scorn any attempt to discredit her.

'Come off it, Zac.' Dana could hear her now. 'She can't be the first girl who's come on to you and the others have all been old enough to know better. Besides, it was a long time ago.'

A long time ago, she repeated silently. So why did it feel as if it were only yesterday?

And what if he replied, 'But it wasn't me she wanted. Not then. Not now. It's Adam—and this house.'

He could blow her plans clean out of the water with one sneering remark. Could—and probably would.

Her legs were shaking, but she dragged every rag of calm she possessed around her, to get her safely up the steps.

But not past him…

He was standing, hands on hips, his face a mask, his eyes raking her from head to foot, as he said softly, 'So you have come back. I thought you would have more sense.'

Dana met his gaze, hard as obsidian. 'I accepted an invitation from an old friend, nothing more.' She lifted her chin. 'And how are things with you, Mr Belisandro? Still devouring the world?'

'In small bites, Miss Grantham.' His voice was a drawl, his tone tinged with ice. 'And never more than I can comfortably chew. A policy I recommend to you, *signorina*.'

The close-fitting charcoal pants he wore had

the sheen of silk, while the matching shirt was negligently unbuttoned revealing more of the muscular bronze of his chest than she'd any wish to see.

It made her feel uneasy—almost restless, and she shrugged, fighting to regain some equilibrium. 'That depends, I suppose, on the size of one's appetite.'

'And yours, if memory serves, borders on the voracious. If you wish to discuss mine, I suggest we choose somewhere more private. The summer house, perhaps.'

He watched the swift flare of colour in her face and nodded, smiling a little. 'So this new sophistication is only skin-deep after all. But how fascinating. And what temptation.'

'I'd say—what arrogance, Mr Belisandro.' Her hands curled into fists at her sides. 'You clearly haven't changed at all.'

It wasn't true. He'd matured, wearing his thirty-two years with toned grace. He'd always been attractive. Even she had to admit that. But now he was—spectacular. And, as such, formidable.

'I have never found a reason to do so,' he said. 'Although I may have become a little more compassionate than I was seven years ago, so let me offer you some advice.'

He took a step towards her and it needed every scrap of self-command she possessed not to back away.

He went on quietly, 'Recall some pressing engagement and return to London. Meet Nicola for lunch occasionally, if both of you so wish. But hope for nothing more. That way you may remain unscathed.'

He paused. 'Continue on your present path, and you will regret it.'

Her throat tightened but she managed a little laugh. 'How very melodramatic. Is this how you threaten your business competitors?'

'I rarely find it necessary. They listen to reason. I suggest you do the same.'

'Thank you.' Dana drew a deep breath. 'Please believe that if ever I need your advice, I'll ask for it. In the meantime, I plan to enjoy a pleasant weekend in these beautiful—and desirable—urroundings. I hope you do the same.'

'If you're looking for Adam,' he said as she turned towards the French windows. 'He has not yet arrived. He is driving down with his latest girl, Robina Simmons, whose lack of punctuality is legendary, so they have probably quarrelled.' He smiled. 'Let us hope the disagreement will not last.'

'Unlike ours,' Dana threw over her shoulder. 'Which I'm sure will run and run.'

Not much of a last word, she thought shakily, but better than nothing.

The drawing room was empty so she was able to escape to her room without another unwanted confrontation to add to the inner turmoil, already threatening to tear her apart.

Zac Belisandro—here, she thought as she sank down on the edge of the bed. How was it possible? And why hadn't Nicola warned her?

Because she had no reason to do so, she answered her own question. To Nicola, Zac was simply Serafina's billionaire cousin and Adam's friend. Someone she'd known and trusted for most of her life.

Whereas to me, she thought bitterly, he's the man who's already tried to ruin my life once, and who hasn't finished yet. He's made that more than clear.

Just as he'd relished telling her that Adam

wasn't arriving alone, although she wouldn't let herself worry too much about that. According to his sister he had a rapid turnover in girlfriends—and if they were already quarrelling...

"Adam wanted me once," she whispered to herself. "I have to make him remember that—and want me again, even more. To the point of desperation, no less. Because only he can give me Mannion, and I'll settle for nothing less."

Not that he would have any reason to feel shortchanged. She would make him a good wife—the best—and be the perfect hostess in a house she would restore to its former glory.

Even Zac Belisandro would have to admit as much...

She paused right there, shocked at herself, her heart skipping a nervous beat.

Because what did his opinion matter—or his empty threats? His presence here was temporary. His work—his life—belonged thousands of miles away and soon he would be returning there to resume both of them.

While she would still be here. So why was she letting him get to her—invading her consciousness even marginally?

She drew a deep, steadying breath.

She'd waited so long for this day when she'd finally return to Mannion that it was hardly surprising she found herself on edge, making mountains out of what would prove to be molehills.

What she needed now was to relax—and regroup.

A warm bath would be good, followed by a brief nap before she dressed for dinner.

Tonight's outfit had been chosen with care, because she needed to make it count. It was a simply cut dress in a silky and striking fabric the colour of amber, which added lustre to her skin, while the low square neck, revealing the first creamy swell of her breasts and the brief flare of the skirt was gently but enticingly provocative.

She had amber drops set in gold for her ears—a present to herself bought from her first bonus at Jarvis Stratton, to mark the moment when she'd thought of herself as having a career instead of just a job. When she'd started to believe in herself again, and feel a growing conviction that she would succeed where her mother had failed.

When conviction had become stony determination.

Not that marrying Adam would impose any kind of hardship, she mused, as she made her way to the bathroom. On the contrary, it could be an additional perk.

As she lay in the scented water, she looked down at her body, examining it as if it belonged to a stranger. Trying to judge it through a stranger's eyes. A man's eyes.

Wondering what Adam would think the first time he saw her naked. When she allowed that to happen.

Asking herself too if he would be glad to find her still innocent and know that she had kept herself for him.

It was a decision that had caused problems with the men she'd dated during the past seven years. A few had been bewildered, some hurt and most of them angry when they discovered that her 'no' meant exactly that. 'Commitment-phobe' had been one accusation. 'Frigid' had been another.

But Adam would have no reason to say that, she told herself as she stepped out of the bath, reaching for a towel.

She smoothed body lotion in her favourite scent into her skin, aware how close to her a man, intrigued by its subtle fragrance, would need to be in order to appreciate it fully.

And she intended Adam to get pretty damned close, no matter how many girlfriends he might have in tow. Because she would be the one who would count.

She was back in her room applying a final coat of mascara to her lashes when Nicola came knocking at the door.

She looked around her, pulling a face. 'Dana, I'm so sorry about this. When Zac announced he'd be joining us, Aunt Mimi had a panic attack and gave him the room I'd picked for you. And we're pretty full up, so I can't really move you.'

'It's fine. Don't worry about it.' Dana returned her cosmetics to their purse. She kept her voice casual. 'So you weren't expecting him?'

'Well, eventually, just not this weekend. But his father was having heart surgery which got re-scheduled, and he flew back early to be around for the operation.' She smiled. 'Apparently it was a great success. He must be so relieved.'

I didn't see many signs of rejoicing, thought Dana, examining her flawless nails.

'And he didn't feel obliged to rush back and

make sure Belisandro Australasia hadn't collapsed in his absence?' she queried drily.

'Oh, he's not going back to Melbourne,' said Nicola with appalling cheerfulness. 'From now on he'll be based in Europe, waiting to take over as chairman of the whole shebang when his father retires, which might be quite soon. And he'll be working from London, so we'll see much more of him.'

For a moment Dana felt the room sway about her. 'I see,' she managed.

She swallowed. 'How—how did the visit to the church go?'

'Brilliantly. The country wedding is definitely on, although I don't know what Dad will say.'

Dana's brows lifted. 'He's coming, then, to give you away?'

Nicola sighed. 'Yes, and bringing the ghastly Sadie with him unfortunately.'

Diverted momentarily from her own troubles, Dana gave her a sympathetic look. That first sailing holiday had turned life upside down for Adam and Nicola. Francis Latimer had decided he'd found his true metier, and to the shock of the entire family, he'd thrown up his safe city job and bought a struggling sailing and diving venture in the Greek islands, which by sheer hard work and force of will, he'd turned into a roaring success.

Along the way, he'd met Sadie, an Australian working for one of the large tour companies supplying him with excursion business, and a summer fling had continued throughout the winter and thereafter.

Sadie was loud, determinedly jolly and convinced she would soon have her Frankie's children eating out of her hand. When it didn't happen, she became increasingly resentful and family holidays turned into a hostile nightmare.

Which was how Nicola, and Adam too, had come to pass the greater part of their school vacations at Mannion, while their father spent his winters in Queensland, running a boat chartering business with Sadie's brother Craig.

'Well, at least you're seeing him again.' Dana tried to sound consoling. 'Have you heard from your mother?'

'An occasional letter telling us she's happy and staying where she is. How about you?'

Dana forced a shrug. 'Much the same, although the information filters through from Aunt Joss.'

Apparently Linda found her daughter too strong a reminder of everything that had gone wrong in her life for direct contact, and Dana had been advised to accept that and let her find her own way back. If she ever did.

But if I can offer her Mannion, she thought, then maybe I'll discover the mother I've never really known. The one with hopes and dreams who existed before Jack Latimer was killed. Not the woman disowned by his mother and left out on a limb to grieve with no way back, but the smiling, pretty girl who'd helped run the Royal Oak because the landlord's wife drank.

'Life and soul of the place, she was,' Betty Wilfrey, the Royal Oak's cook had once told her. 'Reception, bar work, chambermaiding, she could turn her hand to anything. It was never the same after she left. No wonder Bob Harvey sold up and went too before a year passed.'

And now all too many years had gone by, thought Dana. Her throat tightening, she got to her feet. 'Should we go down?'

'I guess so. Dinner's running slightly late because Adam's only just arrived, in a bit of a strop and without Robina, because they've had a fight,' said Nicola, adding with a touch of grimness, 'I've had to remind him that this is my weekend, not his.'

Dana bit her lip. 'Perhaps he's upset because he really does care for her,' she suggested reluctantly.

'Adam cares for getting his own way,' Nicola said shortly as they left the room.

Pre-dinner drinks turned out to be champagne on the terrace, poured, Dana saw, by Zac Belisandro, immaculate in a dark grey suit with a silk tie the colour of rubies.

As Dana accepted her flute with a murmur of thanks, she was acutely aware of his gaze slowly examining her, lingering on the roundness of her breasts.

His unashamed scrutiny revived memories she wanted very badly to forget, and she was glad to obey Nicola's summons and greet her former schoolmates Joanna and Emily, with their respective fiancés.

Then Eddie was commandeering her to meet his parents, a handsome grey-haired couple, radiating contentment about their son's engagement and openly—sweetly—about each other.

They were also with patient goodwill listening to Mimi Latimer bewailing Robina's no-show and its detrimental effect on the *placement* at dinner.

'It can hardly matter,' Mrs Marchwood said soothingly. 'Not at a family dinner when we're all friends.'

Miss Latimer acquiesced reluctantly, but the look she sent Dana told a very different story.

But what did that matter when Adam had just appeared on the terrace, smiling and relaxed in a cream linen suit and an open-necked shirt as blue as his eyes, any earlier bad humour apparently forgotten or put on hold?

He saw Dana and stopped short, his eyes widening.

'My God, I don't believe it.' He turned to his sister. 'Nic, you little devil, so this is the surprise you promised me.'

He crossed to Dana, taking both her hands in a graceful gesture and laughing down into her face.

'Where on earth did you spring from—after all this time? How long is it, exactly?'

She could have told him to the day, the hour, the minute, but was saved from temptation by Mimi Latimer.

'She's been selling overpriced flats in London, one of them to Nicola and Edward, it seems. I hope they have a survey done.'

'A full one—before they made their offer,' Dana said crisply. 'Hello, Adam. It's good to see you.'

'So, you're a career girl.' Adam shook his head. 'I often wondered what had become of you.'

Then why didn't you try to find me...?

But she didn't ask the question aloud. Instead she smiled back at him, keeping her tone casual. 'Oh, I've never been that far away. And I can't tell you how it feels to be here again—with all these memories.'

'More champagne?' said Zac Belisandro blandly, appearing beside them as silently as a dark ghost and refilling the glass she'd put down on a table. 'To celebrate this joyous reunion.'

Hoping I'll drink too much and make a fool of myself, no doubt, she thought as she gently removed her hands from Adam's clasp. But it's not going to happen, because this top-up is going to be poured away as soon as Zac's back is turned.

Except, that never seemed to happen. He wasn't

actually following her. He was just—never very far away.

But then, when had he ever been?

But this weekend she would deal with it. She might not be able to distance herself physically, or not until she was the mistress of the house and could control the guest list, but she could and should excise him mentally once and for all.

Put the events of seven years ago in a box, close it securely, then let it drop from thirty thousand feet into the Mariana Trench or some other abyss. Wasn't that what the therapists recommended?

It might not have worked for my mother, she thought bitterly, *but I'll damned well make it work for me.*

She took judicious sips of champagne during the chilled cucumber soup and the poached fillets of sole, accepting half a glass of claret to accompany the beautifully roasted ribs of beef.

She'd been seated between Greg and Chris, the bridesmaids' fiancés, well away from Adam who occupied the head of the table, but perfectly placed to hear the chunterings of Miss Latimer, stationed at its foot.

'Such a shame dear Robina can't be with us,'

she declared fretfully during a lull in the general conversation, adding, to Adam's obvious displeasure, 'I know lateness can be trying, but I understand even the dear Queen Mother was habitually unpunctual in her younger days.'

Dana felt a bubble of laughter welling up inside her. At the same moment, she realised that Zac was looking at her from the other side of the table, his dark eyes brilliant, alight with shared and quite unholy amusement and found her gaze locked with his.

Like being mesmerised, she thought, and a shiver ran through her.

Shocked, she bit her lip hard to break the spell, forcing herself to look down at her plate, knowing as she did so that her remaining appetite had deserted her.

Knowing too that she couldn't permit any kind of connection between them however trivial, however fleeting. Could not afford the slightest threat to her plans.

Chris was speaking to her and she turned to him in relief. 'This is the most amazing house. It's actually got a billiard room. When I went in, I expected to find Professor Plum with the candlestick.' He paused. 'I understand you and Nic grew up here together?'

'Hardly,' Miss Latimer put in tartly. 'Dana's aunt was the housekeeper here.'

'She certainly was.' Dana made herself speak lightly. 'And I believe this is her version of lemon syllabub that we're eating now. She must have left the recipe for her successor.'

'There've been several of those.' Mimi Latimer again. 'It's almost impossible to get reliable help these days. People simply don't know their place any more.'

'I think they do,' Dana returned quietly. 'Only these days they tend to choose their own.'

'Adam was saying there used to be an Orangery,' Greg put in quickly as Mimi bridled. 'Only he's turned it into a swimming pool.'

The Orangery gone, Dana thought, startled. But it had been Serafina's pride and joy. Did she know what Adam intended when she handed over the house? If so, how could she have let it happen?

If I hadn't been sent away—if I'd stayed here with Adam, I wouldn't have let him do it, she thought. I'd have talked him out of it somehow.

'Some Orangery,' Adam said, taking another helping of syllabub. 'I never remember a single orange, so I decided a pool would be more useful—and more fun.'

Practical, thought Dana. But depressing. And if something had to go, I wish you'd chosen the summer house.

She shivered again and Chris noticed.

'Feeling cold?' he asked, surprised.

'No, just a slight headache,' she improvised hastily. 'Maybe there's a summer storm on the way.'

And saw in a flash, like the lightning she'd just invented, the sardonic twist of Zac's lips. Telling her the storm was already here—and waiting for her.

CHAPTER THREE

AFTER DINNER, THE PARTY split up, the men going off to the billiard room for a knock-out snooker tournament, and the women congregating in the drawing room for coffee and wedding chat.

Dana had already resigned herself to the knowledge that there'd be no opportunity for a private conversation with Adam. Certainly not while Zac was hovering at his shoulder.

But she was annoyed to discover that her fib about a headache was coming true. That will teach me a lesson, she thought, as she made her excuses and took herself off to bed.

Even with the window open, the small room was stifling, and even lying naked under a single sheet, she felt as if she was suffocating. And her headache was getting worse.

Stress, she thought, searching vainly for a cool spot on the pillow. Tension. That's all it is. And I know exactly who to blame for it.

She swallowed a couple of the ibuprofen she'd found in the bathroom cupboard, and eventually fell into a restless doze only to be woken again by a fierce rumble of thunder directly overhead, accompanied by a waft of cold, damp air and the splash of rain.

I don't believe this, she groaned as she stumbled out of bed, closed the window and put on her cotton nightshirt. What else can I wish upon myself?

And now she'd be awake while the storm lasted, or even for the rest of the night. Just when she needed all her wits about her for the day ahead.

She hadn't brought a book with her, but downstairs in the room which had once been Serafina's study, there'd be the daily paper and a selection of magazines, to provide her with temporary distraction until the night became quiet again.

She put on her robe, tying the sash tightly round her waist and trod quietly along the passage to the stairs.

The house was still, as if she was the only one to be disturbed by the weather. She opened the study door, went across to the desk and switched on the lamp.

'*Buongiorno,*' Zac said courteously.

Dana spun round with a startled cry, her heart thumping.

He was sitting in the high-backed armchair beside the empty fireplace, fully dressed apart from his coat and tie, which were on the floor beside him.

'What are you doing here?' she demanded unevenly.

He got to his feet, raking back his hair with a lazy hand. 'I needed some private time to think, after which I seem to have slept. Until, of course, you whistled up this storm, my little witch, when I stayed to watch nature's light show. It has been quite spectacular. And you? Have you come down to dance between the raindrops?'

'Very amusing.' She picked up the nearest magazine—a county glossy—from the desk. 'Please resume your viewing. I won't disturb you any longer.'

He said quite gently, 'If only that were true. But we both know it is not. Nor that simple.'

'I know nothing of the kind,' she said curtly, aware of his scrutiny and wishing her robe was infinitely thicker. And that she did not have to walk past him to reach the door.

And, more importantly, that she'd stayed safely in her room in the first place.

'Then consider it now.'

As he spoke, another flash of lightning blazed into the room through the uncurtained windows and the lamp on the desk went out, leaving them first dazzled, then in total darkness.

Dana gasped. 'What's happened?'

'A local power cut.' His tone was laconic. 'The storm playing havoc with the electrics. It often happens, as I am sure you remember.'

Yes, she thought, but she hadn't bargained for it to happen here and now.

She said quickly, 'I'd better go back to my room.'

'Why the haste?' He paused. 'After all, we have been alone in the dark before, you and I.'

As if she could have forgotten, she thought shakily. And it was not a situation she could afford to repeat.

He hadn't moved. She would swear to that, but she felt that he was somehow nearer. As if the walls of the room were closing in on them, and she needed to get out—to get away in the same way that she needed to draw her next breath.

She thought, I have to be safe.

She began to edge towards where she thought the door should be, only to catch her foot in something lying on the floor—oh, God, his bloody coat—and stumble forward, her balance gone.

Only to find herself grabbed and steadied, then held in the circle of his arms, feeling his warmth, inhaling the haunting trace of the cologne he still used after all this time. Aware that his grasp was tightening.

Panic closed her throat.

'Let go of me, damn you.' She choked the words then struck upwards, her hands curled into claws, finding taut skin stretched over bone and a hint of stubble.

She felt Zac wince, heard him swear under his breath before he stepped back, freeing her.

Another jagged flash lit up the room, and gathering the folds of her robe in clumsy hands, Dana ran to the door and across the wide hall to the stairs.

She tripped twice, clutching at the smooth oak bannister rail, almost hauling herself, panting, from step to step in case he was there behind her, following silently, cat-like, in the stifling darkness.

Wondering, if his hand fell on her shoulder, if she would have breath enough to scream and what she would say if she did and people came. How she could possibly explain when the real explanation must remain hidden. For ever.

In her room, with the door closed and the key turned in the stiff lock, she picked up the discarded coverlet from the floor and rolled herself in it, pulling a fold over her head and lying still, waiting for her heartbeat to slow and the rasp of her breathing to subside into normality.

But her cocoon provided no protection at all against the soft trembling deep within her, or the thoughts and memories she could no longer exclude from her consciousness, however hard she might try.

And, perhaps, in order to be free, she should allow her mind to travel back over seven years and—remember.

She should not even have been at Mannion that summer. Aunt Joss had visited the school to tell her with faint awkwardness about the planned alternative.

'My friend Mrs Lewis has found you a job through her employment agency. A Mrs Heston needs an au pair to look after her eight-year-old girl and twin boys aged three. You'll live as family and Mrs Heston will make sure you keep up with any holiday work set by the school.'

'But I don't want to spend my vacation with a bunch of strangers,' Dana protested. 'Nicola's expecting me to come home with her. They're having lots of people to stay, and there'll be parties. And it's Adam's birthday.'

'Thank you,' said her aunt. 'But I'm well aware of the social arrangements, as I shall be bearing the brunt of them.'

'If I was there, I could help.'

'I doubt that.' Aunt Joss paused. 'You have been excellent company for Nicola in the past, but you're not children any more and you're going to be leading very different lives, especially when Mrs Latimer's arrangements over the house are complete.'

She meant when Adam took over.

As if Dana didn't know that. As if it hadn't

been at the forefront of her mind since she'd first heard the news that her mother's claim was being passed over yet again.

Something she would never accept.

Lying in her narrow bed at night, her brain seething, she'd invented and rejected all kinds of scenarios, but in the end it always came back to Adam.

She had never expected him to notice her, except as his younger sister's friend and schoolmate, but thanks to Nicola that had changed a couple of years before, when Adam had come down to Mannion with a party of friends during the girls' half-term break, and an impromptu tennis tournament had been organised.

Nicola had immediately turned down Adam's invitation to partner him. 'You should ask Dana,' she'd declared. 'She's in the school team and a hundred times better than I am.'

If Adam was surprised at having the housekeeper's niece foisted on to him, he hid it politely. In gratitude, Dana played out of her skin, and they ended as runners up in the tournament.

'You should have won,' said Zac Belisandro, who'd strolled down to watch the later stages. He looked at Adam. 'You poached too many balls at the net, my friend, and failed to put them away.'

Dana felt a surge of resentment. He might be Serafina's cousin and a ruthless and dynamic business tycoon, but she hated the way he appeared to stroll through life as if it had been created for his private amusement.

He was someone she tried to avoid when he was at Mannion—and he was there a lot.

'It's not Adam's fault,' she said impetuously. 'He knows volleying isn't my strong point and he was trying to protect me.'

There was a silence, then Zac's brows rose. 'Ah,' he said softly. Mockingly. 'So that is how it is.' He turned back to Adam. 'Serafina wishes to remind you there is tea on the terrace.'

'Right, my shield and defender.' Adam slid a casual arm round her shoulders. 'Tea we shall have, and with strawberries and cream, even if this isn't Wimbledon.'

Glowing, she allowed herself to be swept along.

She wasn't invariably his partner that summer or the two that followed, but often enough to count, and to fill her with joyous anticipation at the start of every school holiday, as she waited for his usual visit. Then waited again for him to notice her and smile.

By the time she was seventeen, she was well past any lingering trace of puppy fat, spots or greasy hair. She had changed and so had the way that Adam had begun to look at her, his gaze considering, lingering and filling her with secret excitement.

Because he was acknowledging, she told herself exultantly, that she'd become a woman.

And he'd sealed his discovery by the kiss under the mistletoe they'd shared that Christmas in an unexpected moment of privacy. A kiss that had lengthened. Deepened, hinting at something far more, leaving her breathless.

'My God,' he'd whispered huskily as, reluctantly, they parted. 'You're full of surprises, Dana, my sweet, and I want to explore them all.'

Then, hurriedly, he'd let her go as the sound of voices signalled the end of the moment.

But there would be others. He'd said it and she knew it with a thrill of anticipation. Maybe at Easter…

But Adam did not come to Mannion at Easter.

'He's gone surfing in Cornwall with Zac and some other people,' Nicola had told her casually.

Instinct told Dana that it would not be an all-male trip, but, then, why would it be? She knew through Nicola that he had girlfriends in London although they never accompanied him to Mannion.

'Because Serafina wouldn't let them share a room,' Nicola had confided with a giggle. 'She's very strict about such things. And Adam wouldn't want to upset her—especially now.'

What was so special about now? Dana had wondered, puzzled. And then Aunt Joss had told her about Serafina handing over Mannion, and she'd understood.

Understood and made her plans for the summer accordingly, only to have them completely blown out of the water, so that she could spend eight weeks running around after three children. It didn't bear thinking about.

I need a miracle, she'd told herself.

A visit to the headmistress's office wasn't usually seen in that light, but as she came away Dana felt like cartwheeling down the corridor.

'The Heston girls have got chickenpox and the

whole family is in quarantine because none of them have had it—and neither have I,' she told Nicola jubilantly.

'Oh, thank heaven.' Nicola's face lit up. 'It would have been awful without you. Now, we can have the best summer ever.'

Oh, yes, Dana had told herself. She would make sure of that—with Adam.

How sure I was, she thought now. And how terribly—shamingly wrong.

The storm had moved away into the distance, with only an occasional faint rumble as a reminder. She left the bed and walked to the window, drawing the rush of air deep into her lungs. She pulled over the solitary chair and sat, resting folded arms on the sill, looking out into the darkness. Still no lights anywhere. No moon. Not even the glimpse of a star.

And yet she could see the summer house as clearly as if it had been floodlit. Or simply imprinted on her mind in every detail.

Wooden, she thought, with a thatched roof and verandah where Serafina's rattan lounger and footrest stood, because the summer house with its view over the house and grounds was her special place.

Thick wooden shutters over unglazed windows, and a wide door opening outwards. Inside, a small table holding a shallow pottery dish containing an assortment of tea lights. Folding chairs against one wall, and facing the door, an enormous elderly sofa, its once luxurious cushions now shabby and sagging, with an equally ancient fur rug on the floor in front of it.

And when she and Nicola had outgrown their shrubbery den, and Serafina did not require it, they were allowed to play there.

Strict rules applied. It had to be left clean and tidy, they were not allowed matches for the tea lights, and they had to close the shutters—'Squirrels,' Nicola had said succinctly—and lock up, taking the key back to the house and its hook in the boot room.

But that had been a small price to pay for all those long ago summer days and endless games of make believe.

And even when their fantasies had changed, they'd still enjoyed the occasional picnic there.

She was looking forward to more of them—

perhaps with Adam, but Aunt Joss had other ideas.

'There's little to be done about chickenpox,' she'd said grimly. 'But I can't have you kicking your heels here for weeks on end, so Mrs Sansom at the Royal Oak has agreed to take you on to help with the rooms and wait at table, although you can't work behind the bar. She'll pay you a small wage and you can keep any tips. Your shift will finish once the lunchtime bar snacks are over.'

Dana had listened, appalled. Even the thought of earning some money of her own couldn't reconcile her to being Mrs Sansom's dogsbody for half a day. 'She likes a big cake for her ha'penny' as a local saying had it.

Worse, Janice Cotton who'd been the leading bully when she was at the village school was working in the Oak's kitchen, and would almost certainly be waiting to put the boot in.

And if, by some ghastly mischance, Adam and his friends ever decided on a bar lunch in the garden, she'd have to serve them wearing a hideous pink overall with a bright green oak tree emblazoned on the left breast.

And I thought being an au pair was the pits, she'd groaned inwardly.

But she seemed to have little choice in the matter, so the following morning saw her cycling to the village, where, as bad luck would have it, the first person she encountered was Janice.

'Well, if it isn't Miss High and Mighty,' was the greeting, delivered pugnaciously, hands on hips. 'Tired of your airs and graces up at the big house, are they? Sent you down here, slumming with us peasants? Sorry if I don't curtsy.'

Dana made no reply as she parked her bike, reflecting that biting her lip hard might well become a way of life.

And, as she soon discovered, working her fingers to the bone.

Her initial encounter with Mrs Sansom had not raised her spirits one iota. Her employer, in her own much repeated words, 'liked to run a tight ship'. Her tone suggested that any backslider would soon find they were walking the plank.

The Oak did a brisk bed and breakfast trade and the changeover in its six bedrooms had to be swift and efficient.

Theoretically, the rooms had to be vacated by

10:00 a.m., but this didn't happen as often as it should, and it generally became a mad rush to get the laundry downstairs in time for the van, dust and polish the lounge bar and mop its flagged floor, check the garden parasols and check the ashtrays were clean before washing her face and hands, tidying her hair and changing into a clean pink overall for her waitress stint.

At the same time, she had to contend with Janice, who had soon made her malicious intentions clear, focusing on the hated uniform.

It seemed hardly a day went by without some accident, a favourite being a jog to her arm as she was pouring breakfast juice or ladling soup into bowls, necessitating a change of overall, which could have its own problems.

'You really are the clumsiest girl,' Mrs Sansom snapped when Dana had to show her the only clean overall she had left, with a sleeve mysteriously hanging half torn from the armhole. 'How on earth did that happen?'

'I don't know, Mrs Sansom,' said Dana, although she could make an educated guess at the kitchen scissors followed by a good, hard tug.

'Well, I suppose you must serve in your own

clothes for once, but be more careful in future or I shall have to speak to your aunt. These uniforms cost money, you know, and you're damned lucky I don't deduct this damage from your wages.'

But it turned out to be her lucky day, because the cook, Betty Wilfrey, who'd allowed previous incidents to pass without comment, apparently decided enough was enough and took Janice aside for 'a quiet word'.

For a week or two there was peace; then, after a long, weary day with the temperature up in the eighties, the hotel full and the busiest lunchtime ever, Dana emerged later than usual and well after the kitchen had closed, to find that her bike had disappeared from its usual spot.

'I don't believe it,' she groaned under her breath. She hoped it might just have been moved elsewhere, but a search of the outbuildings and storage area proved futile and Dana could have sat down on the cobbles, put her face in her hands and wept.

It was no use trudging the half mile to the small estate where Janice lived, because she would only deny all knowledge of the incident. So, instead,

Dana turned left and began to walk the length of the village, cursing Janice with every step.

She'd coped with the odd flat tyre in the past and said nothing, but this was different. This time she couldn't suffer in silence—not with the prospect of a three-mile hike at the beginning and end of every working day.

She'd gone about half a mile when she was overtaken by a dark blue convertible, which stopped.

'Good afternoon,' said Zac Belisandro. 'Isn't it a little warm for a stroll?'

'I didn't plan it.' She stared ahead of her fixedly, one glance having told her that he was more casually dressed than she had ever seen him, bare-legged and bare-armed in white shorts and a dark red shirt unbuttoned almost to the waist.

'You have a bicycle, I think.'

Now, how did he know that?

'I couldn't find it. Someone must have—borrowed it.'

'Without permission?'

She shrugged. 'Obviously. Anyway, the walk will do me good.' Even if my feet feel as if they're about to burst into flames.

'I disagree.' He leaned across and opened the passenger door. 'Get in.'

Oh, God, no...

She said swiftly, 'No, thanks, I can manage. You really don't have to bother.'

'It will only trouble me if I am forced to put you in the car.' He sounded faintly bored. 'For both our sakes, do as you are told.'

The desire to tell him to go to hell almost overwhelmed her. Almost—but not quite.

So she obeyed, a picture of mutiny, fastening her seat belt quickly in case he offered assistance again.

He added, 'And do not sulk.'

'Does it occur to you that I might not wish to be driven by you, Mr Belisandro?' She'd intended to sound dignified, but somehow the words emerged as juvenile and petulant.

His own tone was silky. 'Then it is fortunate we have only a short journey to endure.' He paused. 'Besides, I am not convinced that you yet know what you truly want. I also believe you should be careful what you wish for.'

The car moved forward and began to gather speed. The languid heat of the day seemed suddenly to be pulsing in Dana's veins and, in spite of herself, she lifted her face welcoming the rush of air.

'I've simply mislaid my bike,' she returned. 'I hardly require counselling.'

'Is that what I'm offering?' His mouth twisted in the way that always put her on edge. 'I believed it was kindness, but perhaps you have little reason to recognise it.'

'But I do know, however, when I'm being patronised,' Dana said stonily.

'Then let us change the subject. Do you know who has your bicycle?'

'I think—Janice Cotton who works in the pub kitchen. I—I expect she meant it as a joke.'

'She has a strange sense of humour.' His tone was dry.

'Well, that's the English for you.' She attempted airiness. 'Unpredictable.'

'You include yourself in that category?'

'Why not?'

He said softly, 'Because I can already foresee the future you have chosen for yourself. The decision you have made to remain anchored to the ground when you could fly.'

Dana stiffened. 'I don't know what you're talking about.'

'*Che peccato.* What a pity. Yet again totally predictable.'

She said huskily, 'You know nothing about me. Nothing. So what gives you the right to speculate?'

'Aesop wrote a fable about a little dog who, through greed, mistook fantasy for reality and lost what was most precious to him.' He paused. 'I would not wish you to trade your substance for a mere shadow, Dana *mia.*'

In the taut silence which followed, the car reached the crest of the hill and Dana saw Mannion waiting below, so familiar, so perfect, so desirable.

My substance, she thought. No matter what I have to do to get you and keep you.

She said, her voice shaking, 'I don't believe in fables, Mr Belisandro. If I make mistakes, I'll stand by them and the last thing I need is advice from you.'

She added fiercely, 'And I am not *your* Dana.'

He said something softly under his breath, and after that there was silence.

It was only when she was safely back in the flat and in her room, that it occurred to her that the whispered words had been 'Not yet.'

Except it couldn't possibly be that, she told herself, dry-mouthed. It couldn't be.

And she wouldn't let herself think about it any more.

CHAPTER FOUR

AUNT JOSS HAD stared at her. 'You can't find your bicycle? What nonsense and typical of your slap-dash approach to life, which Mrs Sansom has already mentioned to me.

'Well, you'll just have to get up an hour earlier and walk. And after work tomorrow, you get the bus to town and see what cycles Shaw have in their secondhand section, and let it be a lesson to you.'

As if, Dana thought wearily, I haven't had enough lessons for one day.

She had money saved but she'd planned to spend it on new clothes, something more fashionable than those her aunt thought suitable, with an outfit for Adam's birthday party heading her list. She needed a pair of high-heeled sandals, and a top to complement the brief flared skirt with its white flowers on a dark green background that she'd produced in sewing class the previous term.

She'd also hoped to visit the town's smartest hair salon for a complete restyle, instead of the usual boring trim by the village hairdresser.

All of it now in abeyance through no fault of her own.

The encounter with Zac Belisandro had shaken her badly too, and telling herself endlessly that everything he'd said was pure speculation didn't help one little bit.

Oh, why couldn't it have been Adam driving from the village instead? Except being discovered at the side of the road hot, tired and sweaty, with her hair escaping untidily from the ponytail Mrs Sansom insisted on was hardly the image she wanted him to have of her.

Working at the Oak didn't leave her the time or the energy for tennis, or very much else, so she needed some other way to put herself back in the frame for him.

His birthday party in ten days' time, when Serafina would hand over Mannion was the obvious opportunity to make him notice her again and remember the pleasure of that mistletoe kiss. To make him want more…

But how much more? What could she find in

her vast ocean of inexperience to keep him intrigued and interested without necessarily 'going all the way' as she knew many of the other girls at school had already done?

The last thing she wanted was for Adam to think she was easy or cheap.

On the contrary, she had, somehow, to make him fall in love with her so deeply that nothing else mattered.

That was the goal. Now she had to find the route and nothing and no one, especially Zac Belisandro, could be allowed to deflect her.

In fact, she wouldn't give him another thought.

That was until she emerged from the flat the following morning, an hour earlier for the expected hike to work and found her bicycle propped against the wall outside with a brand new padlock and chain dangling from the handlebars, and a note taped to the saddle.

For a moment Dana stood transfixed, an inexplicable mixture of emotions going to war inside her as she read the words, 'With my compliments. Z.B.'

How the hell had he managed this? she raged inwardly, screwing the slip of paper to an angry ball in her hand. And now, she supposed, she would have to seek him out at some juncture to thank him. The thought had her screaming silently.

Unless she attached an equally brief response to the steering wheel of his car. Or would he take that as an indication that she was running scared—unwilling to face him?

Well, she wasn't having that, so she would set her teeth and express some form of polite gratitude for his help, even though she'd have preferred to walk ten miles in tight shoes and the heat of the day than do any such thing.

As he'd almost certainly know, she thought grimly, stowing the padlock and chain in her backpack. Was that why he'd gone to all this trouble—simply to put her on the back foot?

I believed it was kindness.

His words of the day before echoed in her head, but she hadn't bought that the first time around and she rejected it utterly now.

She'd heard Nicola speak with awe of his wealth, his success, and the power he exerted. That above all.

Kindness had never been mentioned, and

it wasn't a quality she would ever attribute to that cool, dark, distant figure moving, quiet and watchful, on the edge of their lives.

Which made the retrieval of her bicycle nothing more than a demonstration of that power, reduced to a microcosm.

Reminding her of something else, even more disturbing.

'*I am not* your *Dana.*'

'*Not yet.*'

If that was indeed what he'd said. She still couldn't be sure, so the best thing she could do was put it out of her mind altogether—and go to work.

Surprisingly, it turned into a relatively tranquil day. Janice had called in sick, so any confrontation there had to be postponed.

And what a relief not to have to watch my back all the time, Dana thought. At least, not at work…

Not at Mannion either, she discovered when she got back that afternoon, because Zac Belisandro was no longer there. He'd returned to London, but the bad news was that Adam had gone with him.

She'd learned that from Nicola, who was waiting eagerly for her return armed with a copy of the latest Disney release.

'Serafina's going out,' she said. 'And she's told Cook we can order in pizza if we want.'

'Wow,' said Dana, aware this was a major concession. 'All that plus Johnny Depp. Fantastic.'

Television viewing was confined to a small room at the rear of the house, known as 'the snug'.

Curled up on its sofa, they'd enjoyed the film and were just settling down to cans of Coke and their pizzas—Hawaiian for Nicola and double pepperoni for Dana—when the door opened and Adam came in.

'So this is where you're hiding. I thought the place was deserted.'

'And I thought you were staying in London,' said Nicola.

'I changed my mind. I must have smelt the pizza.'

He sat down between them. Reaching down into the boxes, grabbing a slice from each of them and wolfing them down in a couple of bites.

'Hey, you've had dinner already,' Nicola protested indignantly.

He pulled a face. 'A business thing and hours ago. Besides, you can't talk seriously and eat.'

Nicola's glance was faintly anxious. 'How did it go?'

He shrugged. 'It went. Now, be a love and get me a beer.'

Left alone with him, Dana tensed. This was a chance she couldn't let slip—if only she knew how to use it.

Adam made another dive for the box at her feet. 'Watch out,' he said. 'Or I'll eat it all.'

'It's OK,' she said quickly. 'I'm not very hungry.'

'You can't be on a diet.' His eyes studied her, smilingly at first, then growing more intent. 'Or you might disappear altogether. And that would be a tragedy.'

His gaze moved down. Paused. 'You've missed a bit.'

She glanced down, and saw, mortified, that a slice of pepperoni was adhering to the front of her tee shirt.

Before she could remedy the situation, Adam reached out and took it, his fingers lingering for an instant on the swell of her breast before he popped the fragment of meat into his mouth and swallowed it.

'Delicious,' he said, grinning. 'But then I can never resist—pepperoni.'

She was lost for words, aware only of the hot wave of colour sweeping up from her toes to her hairline.

'God but you're lovely,' he said softly. 'I'd almost forgotten girls could blush.'

He bent towards her and, flustered, she knew he was going to kiss her and couldn't decide how she should react. But with his lips a breath away from hers, they heard Nicola returning and Adam, in one swift movement, reached for another slice of pizza and transferred himself to the other end of the sofa, his swift conspiratorial smile conveying reassurance and a promise.

'Serafina's car is coming up the drive,' Nicola announced as she entered.

Adam grimaced again and got to his feet, hurriedly finishing the pizza. 'Then I'd better postpone the beer until I've made my report.'

'Report?' Dana queried as she and Nicola took the empty cans and boxes to the kitchen.

Nicola nodded glumly. 'Adam's PR company's

in trouble and may have to be wound up. Clients are cutting back because of the recession. But there could be an opening for him at Belisandro Europe, so tonight's dinner was basically a job interview.'

She sighed. 'He'll have to take it, but he'll find it hard after being his own boss.'

Dana felt jolted. Poor Adam, she thought, if he has to end up taking orders from Zac Belisandro.

And the realisation that such a job would mean an even stronger connection between Mannion and the Belisandro family also preyed on her mind as she walked back to the flat to tell Aunt Joss that she'd had a lovely evening.

She was still not sure about the little white top. Each time she tried it on, it seemed to get smaller, skimming her breasts just above the nipples and finishing well short of her midriff, making it impossible to wear a bra.

But the sandals had taken most of her money, so this had been all she could afford. And it hadn't looked nearly so revealing on the market stall.

She could imagine what Aunt Joss would say

if she ever saw it, so she'd have to make sure that 'if' never became 'when'.

And, anyway, it was Adam's reaction that really mattered, she reminded herself defensively.

Since pizza night, he'd become a more frequent visitor at Mannion, where naturally there was business to discuss, but that was clearly not his sole motive and Dana had to be careful that her new glow did not become too obvious.

Adam was careful too, their meetings consisting of snatched moments. Murmured words. Brief kisses.

Which, she told herself, was enough when she had the promise of so much more.

She smiled secretly to herself, recalling how she'd asked him the previous night what he wanted for his birthday, and how he'd smiled at her before whispering, 'Sweetheart, I think you already know.'

And tonight at the party, somehow he would arrange for them to be alone together. She had his word for that.

Contemplating such a step into the unknown was disturbing—even scary. But her ultimate goal was still clear, and if this was what it took...

Taking a deep breath, she removed the white top, placed it on a hanger with the green skirt and hid them both under one of her school dresses in the wardrobe.

And just in time too, because Aunt Joss was calling to her and Dana just had time to slip on her dressing gown before her door opened.

'So there you are,' her aunt exclaimed. 'Why aren't you dressed?'

'I felt so hot and sticky, I decided to have a shower and wash my hair.'

'Well, please be quick. The Vicar will be here in half an hour.'

'Mr Reynolds? Why?'

'His daughter and her husband are staying at the Vicarage, and they're all coming to the party, but the babysitter has let them down at the last minute, so Mrs Latimer suggested you could step in and look after Tim and Molly.'

'But I can't.'

Her aunt's eyes narrowed. 'I hope you have no foolish ideas about attending the party yourself, because you can put that right out of your head. There is a strict guest list and if Nicola has invited you, it was wrong of her, and Mrs Latimer will not be pleased.' She paused. 'So, hurry and have your shower, and make yourself useful instead.'

Just like that, Dana raged inwardly as the warm water cascaded over her a few minutes later. All her hopes and plans swept away—and there was nothing she could do about it. Nothing.

'This is good of you, my dear.' Mr Reynolds's kind face was anxious. 'I know you'd rather be out with your friends, so we're doubly grateful.

'The children are already asleep,' he went on. 'They don't usually wake up or fuss. And we won't be staying too late at the party.' He smiled. 'Tomorrow's my busy day.'

Dana smiled back, reflecting he was not to blame for the collapse of her plans.

At any other time, an evening in the Vicarage's comfortable, shabby sitting room with a generous chunk of Mrs Reynolds's justly famous pork pie, a bowl of home grown tomatoes and a dish of strawberries, also from the garden, waiting on a tray, might have seemed a welcome break with routine, she acknowledged with a soundless sigh. But not tonight.

'I'm not expecting any calls,' Mr Reynolds said as they were leaving amid more expressions of gratitude. 'But I've left a note of my mobile number beside the phone just in case.'

Dana nodded. 'Well—I'll see you later,' she said, knowing she lacked the nobility to hope they'd have a wonderful time.

She'd had supper and was watching an Agatha Christie repeat on television when the telephone rang.

'The Vicarage. Good evening,' she said, reaching for the pencil and pad.

'Good evening,' a familiar voice returned. 'Am I speaking to the babysitter?'

She gasped. 'Adam?'

'Who else? Just to remind you we still have a date, only later than planned. I suggest the summer house. When old Reynolds brings you back, get hold of the key and I'll meet you there, although it may be gone midnight before I can get away.'

He paused. 'Hang on a minute. 'His voice faded as if he'd turned away, and she thought she could hear someone else speaking in the background, then Adam again, his voice impatient. 'Yes, OK, I'll be right with you.'

'Sorry about that.' He was back with her. 'Any chance your aunt will miss you?'

'I'll say goodnight to her. Tell her I have a headache.'

He laughed. 'Just don't use the same excuse with me, sweetheart.' He became brisk. 'At the summer house, leave the key on the inside and don't open the shutters, or someone might see and wonder. Do you like champagne?'

'I've never had any.'

'Ah,' he said softly. 'Another first. I can hardly wait.'

Dana replaced the receiver slowly and looked at herself in the hall mirror, lips parted, eyes bright with a mixture of excitement and apprehension.

Suddenly it all seemed to be moving too far and too fast, with Adam taking much more for granted than she'd expected. And she was not sure she was ready for—that.

I'll deal with it somehow, she thought, swallowing. Because I can't turn back now. There's too much at stake. So, I'll just have to keep him on a string—make him love me—commit himself.

She'd set herself a mountain to climb, but to-night she would take the first step.

She was far too early for their rendezvous, but she'd been too restless to wait at the flat. For one thing she was afraid she might chicken out. For another she was worried her aunt might return unexpectedly and find her up and dressed in the party gear she'd opted for after all.

She'd taken a spare bedspread from the linen cupboard and placed it, rolled up, in her bed which should be enough to deceive any casual glance from the doorway.

There was no moon, so it was lucky she knew the path to the summer house so well, particularly in her new sandals.

The pulsating rhythm from the disco had been replaced by something slow and dreamy, indicating the evening was nearing its end, and that people would be dancing wrapped closely together. Adam probably among them.

But then, he would be coming to her, and she must focus solely on that.

She unlocked the door and slipped inside, fitting the key into the lock as instructed. It disturbed her to discover just how dark it was with both the door and window shutters closed, but Adam would soon be with her, so there was nothing to fear.

She made her way cautiously to the sofa, kicked off her sandals and curled up in a corner against the sagging cushions.

Time passed with aching slowness. The air was still and warm, pressing down on her as heavy as a blanket in the pitch black. It was quiet too without the music from the disco, and Dana began to feel actually drowsy, having to make a conscious effort to keep her eyes open.

Even so, she missed the precise moment of his arrival. It was the faint rasp of the key turning, locking them in together, which jolted her upright, her heart thudding.

She said with a little gasp, 'Oh, you're here at last. Why have you locked the door?'

The only reply was a soft laugh, which could have meant anything, when what she needed was reassurance.

She sensed movement rather than being able to see it. Breathed a trace of fragrance, musky and expensive, in the air.

It was almost like being blindfolded and having to rely on animal instinct.

Then he was there beside her, the warmth of his thigh against hers, his hands on her shoulders, drawing her towards him, and for a moment her taut body resisted, her palms flattened against the crisp frills of his dress shirt.

Because there were things that should be said, and she wanted the candles lit so she could see his face while they were saying them. While, perhaps, they sipped the promised champagne.

She whispered, 'Adam,' and felt his finger touch her lips to hush her.

She realised he was bending towards her. His mouth grazed her hair, her temples, her closed eyes and the curve of her cheek before moving down to her bewildered mouth, brushing it like silk, gentling her into the acceptance—the strange excitement—of his unseen presence. Making her lift her hands to clasp his shoulders. To cling to them.

It was all so different, she thought wonderingly. Almost surreal—like some dark dream she never wanted to end.

He kissed her again, slowly, coaxing her lips

to part for him, so that his tongue could penetrate the moist softness within, sending a shiver of delicious awareness through every nerve ending in her body.

Persuading her to respond, shyly at first and then with growing confidence, growing pleasure, as their tongues tangled, sweetly and sensuously. Showing her how wonderful kissing could be when it didn't have to be hurried. When there was no fear of interruption.

At the same time, his fingertips were stroking the line of her throat, lingering on the curve of her shoulder, then drifting down her back, over the narrow barrier of her top to the silky expanse of warm, bare skin beneath. Where, for an instant, he paused, as if surprised, before continuing his leisurely exploration, his fingers feathering down her spine.

And as Dana gasped and arched involuntarily towards him, she felt him smile against her lips.

He moved then, one arm round her waist, the other under her knees, lifting her, so that she was lying across his thighs, cradled against him.

And he was kissing her again, his lips deepening their demand, as he pulled aside the soft fabric of her top, his hand cupping one small pointed breast, his thumb playing with her nipple, teasing it into erect, aching sensation.

For the first time in her life, Dana was experiencing the full, practised seduction of a man's intimate touch, and she knew that now, if ever, was the time to truly resist. To call a definite halt before her body went into meltdown.

'Adam, you must listen...' Her voice was husky, almost unrecognisable, but once again his only response was the finger laid gently against her parted lips, forbidding further protest.

He found the three pearl buttons that fastened her top and released them before sliding the tiny garment from her shoulders, and discarding it.

Then, bending his head, he took one aroused rosy peak into his mouth, suckling it with delicate hunger, then moved to the other, the erotic flicker of his tongue against her flesh making her moan softly.

She realised in some distant corner of her mind that he was unhooking the waistband of her skirt and removing that too.

And as he kissed her mouth again, his hand began a lingering traverse from her knee along the slender length of her thigh, tracing the edge of her lace briefs with one tantalising finger.

She was too caught up in him, the cool taste of his mouth on hers, the astonishing delight of his touch and the untold pleasures it promised to realise at first that there was a noise.

She was vaguely aware of—something. Some intrusion on the edge of her drowning consciousness. And felt his sudden tension as he heard it too.

Someone was outside, she realised, shocked. Trying the door handle. Rattling it in angry frustration.

'Dana—are you there? Hurry up and open the door, sweetheart.' Adam's voice, pitched low but unmistakable.

For a moment she was still, frozen with disbelief. Because Adam was here with her—making love to her. Wasn't he?

Her throat closed in horror. She began to struggle, but it was useless. She was locked, helpless, in the cage of his arms. Dumb too under the ruthless pressure of his mouth, as it enforced her silence.

'Dana, open the damned door.' Adam was

impatient now. There was a pause, then a thud which might have been a kick at the heavy timbers, followed by a muttered obscenity. And after that—silence, indicating he had gone.

And as she was lifted from the sofa and set on her feet: 'I fear,' Zac Belisandro said lightly, 'that he is a little put out.'

CHAPTER FIVE

SHE FELT AS if she'd been turned to stone, unable to move or to speak. She told herself it was a nightmare. That it had to be, because anything else was impossible. She couldn't have let herself be deceived like this. Couldn't...

And soon she would wake up in bed, at home and safe. Not here in the darkness, whispering, 'Oh, please no—please no' under her breath.

There was the rasp of a match, a brief flare, then, one by one, the tea lights on the table began to burn with a steady flame.

Zac was turning to look at her, his dark eyes glittering mercilessly. Making it all terribly, horribly real.

Reminding her too that while he was still fully dressed, down to his black tie, she was wearing nothing but a few inches of lace.

She snatched up the crumpled skirt lying at her

feet and held it clumsily in front of her, although she knew it was far too late.

Because he had already seen and touched altogether too much, and she knew that, without Adam's arrival, the lace would also have gone, leaving her naked. Knew too that she would never live down the shame at her own stupidity—or the indisputable fact of her body's incredible, unforgivable eagerness to give him anything he might ask.

She didn't recognise herself—this creature subject to her flesh's urgency as if some dam of sensation had been breached by his mouth—his hands.

This man of all men.

When she could speak, she said hoarsely, 'Why? How could you do this?'

He shrugged. 'Why not? You were on offer and charming virgins are a rarity. You can hardly blame me for yielding to temptation when I overheard Adam making this romantic assignation.'

Her voice shook. 'You are totally vile. You disgust me.'

'I am desolated,' he said. 'I thought you were enjoying my attentions.'

'And I was not—on offer.'

'Ah,' he said softly. 'Then you believe you are in love. Well, perhaps you are, but not with Adam.'

'You know nothing about me,' she said stormily. 'Nothing.' And only realised how ridiculous that sounded when he began to laugh.

'I know far more, *mia bella*, than your supposed *inamorato*. And but for his inconvenient interruption, I would have learned everything— so let us not pretend otherwise.'

Rage and humiliation were boiling within her. 'Oh, God, I only wish I could scrape off the skin where you've touched me.'

His mouth twisted. 'An ambition as foolish as it is painful. And impractical. Just be glad you have yet to make the ultimate surrender, and when you do, make sure it is with the right man.' He paused. 'In more ways than one.' His tone became brisk. 'Now get dressed and go home before you are missed.'

As Dana hesitated, his brows lifted. 'Or would you prefer to stay while we explore together the night's infinite possibilities?'

'That's the last thing I want, now or ever. Even before tonight I thought you were loathsome.'

Her voice was breathless in its intensity. 'Do you imagine if I'd known—if I'd had the least idea—that I'd have let you anywhere near me?'

'What a question,' he said. 'And one that perhaps neither of us can answer.

'But now I will ask you something. Why didn't you know I was not Adam? And if your physical acquaintance with him is so limited, why were you here at all?'

'Because he's decent and honourable,' she said defiantly. 'And I trust him.'

'Ah,' he said softly. 'Then there is no more to be said. So put your clothes on and let us bring this little comedy to an end.'

Comedy, she repeated in silent incredulity. He had ruined everything for her and thought it was funny?

She said, 'Not with you watching.'

His ironic glance said it all, but he turned his back while she pulled on her skirt and fumbled with the little pearl buttons. But even when they were safely fastened she felt no more dressed.

Zac did not spare her a second look, busying himself instead with tidying the sofa cushions before unlocking the door and walking back to blow out the tea lights.

When he turned and saw her waiting by the door, his brows lifted. 'Do you wish me to escort you back?' he enquired sardonically. 'And if so can I hope for the usual reward of a kiss?'

'No—on both counts,' she returned curtly. 'You have the key and I need to return it.'

'I shall do that and suggest, perhaps, that it is kept somewhere more secure.' He paused. 'Before you go, Dana *mia*, a word of warning. Mannion is no place for you. You should leave. Set yourself free to find a future elsewhere and begin to live.'

She said thickly, 'Don't you dare tell me what to do. What right have you to interfere—warn me, when by rights, someone should have warned me about you? From now on, stay away from me.'

She turned and walked out into the night, forbidding herself to hurry, aware that her legs were shaking under her and terrified of missing her footing in the darkness in those sandals, because there was no way she could explain a sprained ankle.

There were tears pricking at the back of her

eyes and tightening her throat, but she refused to cry in case he was close enough behind her to hear her distress.

She retrieved her key from the flower tub by the front door and let herself noiselessly into the darkened flat, going straight to her room.

She wanted to have a shower, to wash away his touch, his taste from her body, but she couldn't risk waking Aunt Joss.

Nor could any amount of soap and water cleanse the memory of being in his arms—how he'd made her feel and—worst of all—what he'd made her want.

So she simply stripped, bundling her skirt and top to the back of the wardrobe to be disposed of later, removed the rolled up coverlet and crawled into bed.

Where, at last, she allowed herself to cry with shock—with disappointment and, above all, shame, forcing the corner of the pillow into her mouth to stifle the fierce animal-like sobs.

How could she have thought he was Adam? The question he'd asked her for which she still could find no answer.

'Oh, Adam,' she whispered in total desolation. 'It should have been you. So, why wasn't it? Where were you?'

And eventually, worn out with crying, she fell asleep.

When the alarm woke her, she was almost grateful for the work that would get her away from the house.

Some of the guests from the party were staying at the Oak and enjoying a leisurely Sunday breakfast, so it was almost lunchtime when Dana had finally finished the rooms.

As she lugged the laundry bags downstairs, she found Mrs Sansom waiting for her, unsmilingly, an envelope in her hand.

'Your wages,' she said. 'Which, under the circumstances, is generous. No proper notice. No consideration at all.' She sniffed. 'No doubt this job in London will suit you better.'

'Job in London?' Dana repeated, her mind whirling. 'I don't understand.'

'That's not my concern. I have to find a new assistant from somewhere at my busiest time.' And Mrs Sansom walked back into her office, closing the door with a bang.

Dana had never ridden home so fast in her life. Entering the flat, she saw her school suitcase standing in the hall.

'Come in here, Dana.' Aunt Joss's voice sounded grimly from the kitchen.

She was sitting at the table, her face set.

'What's going on?' Dana asked breathlessly. 'Mrs Sansom's just fired me.'

'No,' said her aunt. 'I rang her and told her you were leaving for London today.'

'But—but why?'

'Because Mrs Latimer will no longer permit you to remain at Mannion.' Miss Grantham's back was ramrod straight. 'To her horror, she has received a serious complaint about you from one of her guests. He has told her that you have been pestering him—embarrassing him by making unwanted and unwarranted sexual advances to him.

'He was reluctant to mention it, but felt your behaviour was placing you at risk, and should be dealt with.

'So, you are to leave immediately.'

Dana made her way unsteadily to the table and sat down on the opposite chair.

Mannion is no place for you.

His words were beating at her brain. Not just a warning, she realised dazedly, but a threat. And now he was using this monstrous lie to get rid of her. To smash her life and her hopes. Because he could…

Aunt Joss was speaking again. 'I thought my sister had caused me enough shame. Hoped you might have learned from her example, but I should have known that the apple never falls far from the tree.' She paused. 'Have you nothing to say?'

It was hard for Dana to speak. Her words seemed to be coming from some bleak bitter abyss.

'It isn't true. He—he's lying.'

Miss Grantham sighed. 'Naturally, you would say so. But why should someone in his position accuse you without foundation? It makes no sense.'

No, thought Dana. It wouldn't—unless she told the whole story. And by admitting she'd agreed to meet Adam in secret, she'd simply be condemning herself in a different way.

As Zac Belisandro knew perfectly well…

'And while I was packing for you, I found these.' She put the green skirt and skimpy top on the table between them. 'Where did they come from?'

'I—I planned to wear them at the party.'

'As a gatecrasher.' Miss Grantham shook her head. 'There's really no more to be said. We'll leave after lunch.'

Dana drew a shuddering breath. 'But this is my home. And what about school? My exams next year?'

'Actions have consequences,' said her aunt. 'Under the circumstances, Mrs Latimer feels totally betrayed and is no longer prepared to fund your education. In future you will have to work for your living.'

She paused. 'The Heston children have recovered from chickenpox and their mother is still desperate to find suitable help. Mrs Latimer has given me the afternoon off to take you to Bayswater and see you settled.'

She added grimly, 'She has no wish to see you before you leave.'

Dana was silent for a moment. 'May I at least say goodbye to Nicola?'

'Her brother is taking her to stay with a friend in Shropshire. You are now considered as an undesirable influence, and required not to contact her in future.' She rose. 'If this seems hard, remember you have only yourself to blame.'

Dana felt sick. 'Only myself?' she repeated under her breath. 'I don't think so. Because now, and for the rest of my life, I shall blame Zac Belisandro.'

And she'd meant what she said. Seven years had passed but she still blamed him. Still hated him for what he'd done. And for what he still might try to do...

Except she was no longer a vulnerable girl to be scared off and dismissed at his whim, but his match and more.

Rehashing the past changed nothing, so from now on she would concentrate her energies on the present and the future. With Adam.

She awoke much too early the next morning, her brain still programmed to working hours. But it was a day worth waking up for, with sunlight and a hazy blue sky promising real heat later.

She took a leisurely bath then, dressed in white linen capri pants and a loose turquoise top, she went quietly downstairs, letting herself out through a side door to make her way round to the terrace.

The air smelt clean and fresh after the rain and the lawns and shrubs sparkled after their dousing.

All's right with the world, Dana thought, drawing a long breath deep into her lungs. Or most of it.

And for a while, Mannion was hers to wander round alone, dreaming as she went.

She moved slowly, breathing the scents from the garden, scanning the facade for signs of decay or neglect, although it seemed to have fared better than the interior.

Although the ivy needed cutting back, she thought critically, wondering if she could mention it to Adam, but deciding that a softly, softly approach would be a better alternative. Taking nothing for granted until it became a certainty.

Smiling, she rounded a corner and realised she'd reached the former Orangery, now the swimming pool. She paused for a moment, contemplating the shimmer of the turquoise water through the glass, noticing how it seemed to be turning to ripples, spreading wider and wider across the surface.

And discovered why as she saw a dark head and the movement of a bronzed arm. The easy turn of a lean, tanned body through the water.

So, she didn't have Mannion to herself after all. There was another early riser.

As she watched, the swimmer reached the side of pool and pulled himself out of the water in one lithe movement.

Naked, Zac Belisandro walked across to a lounger, picked up a towel and began to dry himself.

Dana stood frozen, her heart thudding against her ribs.

Don't let him look round, she implored silently. Don't let him see me.

She began to move backwards, one slow step after another, steadying herself with one hand on the wall until she reached the corner and safety.

She was gasping for breath as if she'd been running, and sank down on her haunches, bending her head and letting her hair fall across her flushed face.

She needed a way to arm herself against the

degrading memories of seven years ago. Now, along with everything else she had to deal with the unwanted image of his lean, sculptured nakedness imprinted on her consciousness.

Calm down, she told herself. Regroup. Concentrate on finding a way to re-establish Adam's interest without alerting the adversary I hoped and prayed I would never see again. Dressed or undressed.

But that was the end of her solitary roam. She couldn't risk being seen, so she would do her thinking elsewhere.

She dashed up to her room to get her bag and minutes later was driving out through the gates. She took the road away from the village which led instead to Rankins Lock.

She parked and walked down to the towpath overlooking the canal. It was very quiet. The half-dozen narrowboats moored there were silent and curtained, but the nearby café was open, already preparing for the breakfast trade.

Maybe some coffee would clear her head and aid coherent thought.

As she walked in, a woman was busy behind the counter and as she straightened, Dana recognised Janice Cotton. Her instinct told her to turn and walk away, but that would be a sign of weakness.

Everywhere I go, I seem to run into the last person I ever want to meet.

'Dana Grantham, of all people. What are you doing back here?'

'Just visiting,' Dana said crisply. 'I'd like coffee, please. Black, filter.'

Janice filled a cardboard beaker from the steaming jug on the hotplate and handed it to her.

'You look as if you're doing all right,' she commented. 'Still with that rich stud you went off with, are you?'

Dana stared at her. 'I don't follow you.'

'The dark dishy guy you sent looking for that manky old bike of yours. Boy, did he get me into trouble with Dad.'

He makes a habit of it, thought Dana, her mouth tightening. She said curtly, 'That was none of my doing. And we certainly didn't leave together because I wouldn't go to the end of the street with him.'

'Well, stroppy or not, I wouldn't have kicked him out of bed, given the chance,' said Janice.

'So, when the pair of you just—vanished like that, people round here put two and two together.'

'Making five plus as usual,' Dana returned crisply. 'And I didn't vanish. I took a job I'd been offered in London. Sorry I didn't put a notice in the paper.'

Janice gave her a long look. 'Stands to reason, he must have fancied you, or why make all that fuss about that old bike.'

Dana's mouth was suddenly dry, but she forced herself to speak more lightly. 'A serious commitment to throwing his weight around, probably. Who knows?' She took out her purse. 'Here's the money for the coffee. I think I'll drink it outside.'

Janice shrugged. 'No skin off my nose.'

Dana's mind was in turmoil as she seated herself on a bench by the towpath.

She supposed it was inevitable that her sudden departure should have caused gossip. Villages were like that. But knowing the talk had linked her with Zac only intensified the old shame and bitterness.

For an instant, she remembered how she'd seen him earlier, lithe as a panther, water beading like crystal on his bare skin.

He must have fancied you...

And, shocked, felt her body stir suddenly at the memories those careless words evoked.

No, she told herself vehemently. It was never that. He was a manipulator—a spoiler who'd wanted her to be sent away, and left her defenceless against his lies.

But this time she knew what he was capable of, and she'd be ready for whatever trick he tried to pull.

Besides, she thought, for Adam she was still unfinished business, which was always a temptation. And she would make him wait—keep him wanting—holding him at arm's length while her smile promised the world.

Zac Belisandro had no weapons to fight that. And this time, he would lose.

She'd expected breakfast to be in full swing when she got back to the house, but, while everyone was certainly assembled in the dining room, 'swing' hardly seemed an appropriate description of the prevailing atmosphere.

Conversation was subdued with Adam seated at the head of the table, his face like stone, and Mimi Latimer at its foot, looking martyred.

The chorus of 'Good morning's which greeted her suggested that her arrival was something of a relief.

Particularly to Nicola. 'There you are,' she exclaimed. 'I took you a cup of tea earlier and wondered where you were.'

'Just revisiting some old haunts.' Nicola helped herself to bacon and scrambled egg from the chafing dishes on the sideboard. 'I'm sorry I'm late,' she added politely to Miss Latimer as she returned to the table, receiving a sniff in return.

She too felt like sniffing when she realised who was sitting opposite.

'You must have been up at the crack of dawn, like Zac,' said Nicola. 'He's already been for a swim this morning.' She shuddered. 'Such energy.'

'Perhaps he likes having the pool to himself,' said Eddie.

'On the contrary,' Zac said softly. 'At one point, I hoped I might have company, but, sadly, it was not to be.'

For a moment, his eyes rested reflectively on Dana, who swiftly lowered her own gaze to her plate, but not before she'd registered the angry mark like a scratch on his cheekbone where she'd struck out at him the previous night.

Good, she thought savagely. I hope you're scarred for life.

Her breakfast had totally lost its attraction but she forced herself to eat, cutting her bacon into very small pieces and wishing that it was Zac under her knife. She was burning with the knowledge that he'd seen her at the Orangery, and, at the same time, aching with the necessity to show no reaction.

Mrs Marchwood leaned forward. 'Working for Jarvis Stratton, Dana, you must meet some fascinating people.'

Dana smiled. 'The job has its moments, but what I enjoy most is matching the person to the property. Finding each client somewhere they're going to love.'

'An estate agent who is also a philanthropist?' Zac queried with deceptive gentleness. 'A unique combination—but we must not forget the commission you earn.'

'I don't,' Dana countered flatly. 'I too need to keep a roof over my head.'

'Was selling property something you always wanted to do, my dear?' Mrs Marchwood again.

Dana shook her head. 'I got into it accidentally while I was still working as a mother's help. My then employers had their house on the market, but were having trouble selling it.'

'Because of the recession?' asked Eddie.

'Partly,' Dana agreed. 'But there were other factors too.'

'Such as?' Emily enquired.

Dana hesitated. Such as the asking price, she recalled ruefully, and presentation. Tess Jameson had not belonged to the blank canvas school of thought and liked her cluttered, untidy, intensely personal house just as it was.

She said carefully, 'I felt that it was the husband who was pushing for a sale, not the wife. Her emotional investment in the house was much greater than his, and she'd made no attempt to detach herself. That can happen a lot.'

'So what happened?' asked Mr Marchwood.

'The family had gone to stay with friends for the weekend, and Jarvis Stratton telephoned on Saturday morning to ask if they could come for an accompanied viewing in the afternoon. I— agreed.

'I tidied round a little,' she went on, glossing over the five frantic hours of decluttering and cleaning, including the bedding and curtains hastily washed, dried and replaced.

'Jarvis Stratton always makes a point of being early, but this time they were late and, after half an hour, the clients were still waiting and getting restless. So, I offered to show them round, and they agreed.'

She shrugged. 'I pretended to myself it was my house, a place I'd loved, where I'd been happy and which I was leaving with regret. And it must have worked, because when the agent turned up, having been stuck in traffic after an accident, the clients were talking seriously about an offer and told him I was a super saleswoman.

'When they'd gone, he gave me his card and a contact name. The following week, I had a job.'

'The girl with the golden touch,' Zac commented sardonically. 'And do you still follow the same policy? Pretending other peoples' houses are yours to love?'

'Why not?' She looked back at him defiantly. 'If it works.'

He nodded. 'So how would you sell Mannion?'

'I wouldn't!' Caught off guard, Dana knew at once she'd made the wrong response. She'd spoken too quickly and vehemently. Made it too personal.

Now she needed to retrieve the situation.

She smiled, shrugging. 'Mannion is a country property which would be handled by a different department in the firm. Sadly, I wouldn't be allowed anywhere near it,' she added, pouring herself some coffee as Zac sat back, his expression ironic.

If this is a duel, she thought, I'd say honours were even. But he nearly drew blood, so I must be careful. So very, very careful.

CHAPTER SIX

DANA WAS THANKFUL when the meal ended and she was able to escape to the terrace where, presently, Nicola joined her.

'What a wonderful start to the day,' she remarked, flinging herself into a chair. 'I don't know which of them I'd like to strangle first, Adam or Aunt Mimi.'

'I thought I detected a whiff of sulphur in the air.' Dana made herself speak lightly. 'What's happened?'

'Aunt Mimi decided to lecture Adam on his role as the owner of Mannion—living up to his responsibilities—settling down—producing a son and heir.' She rolled her eyes expressively. 'She rounded off by urging him, in furtherance of these aims, to make his peace with Robina.

'And Adam, alas, told her very bluntly that he would live his life as he saw fit without any interference from her. Expletives deleted. And all this before the cornflakes.'

She sighed. 'But I'm sorry you had to take the flak. You must have felt you'd been cornered by the Spanish Inquisition.'

'It was fine,' Dana assured her.

'I know Aunt Mimi is tactless and meddling,' Nicola went on. 'But I can't forget how kind she was when the parents were divorcing and things were so awful, taking me to the cinema, the Zoo, Madame Tussauds with tea at Brown's Hotel afterwards.

'Not Adam, of course,' she added bitterly. 'He was far too grown up and superior. He deigned to come to the Natural History Museum once but disappeared halfway through the afternoon. Aunt Mimi was having fits, thinking he'd been abducted or eaten by a dinosaur, but he'd just gone home because he was bored.'

She sighed again. 'And I do worry because Aunt Mimi isn't very well off any more. Her savings and shares have plummeted in value which is why Serafina has let her stay here so often, and it's something she's come to rely on.

'But in a matter of days now, Mannion will belong entirely to Adam, and I'm afraid Aunt Mimi will be toast.'

'Oh, surely not,' Dana said quickly.

'Adam can really bear a grudge.' Nicola shrugged. 'But that's not your problem. I really came to say that we're all going over to Hastonbury Castle—apart from Adam and Zac who are going to play golf—and would you like to come?'

Dana hesitated. 'To be honest, I'd rather stay here. Saturdays are always murder at work and it's such bliss to be able to relax for once.'

'It's your call.' Nicola patted her arm. 'I'll tell Mrs Harris to bring you more coffee and the newspaper. See you later.'

The coffee and paper duly arrived and Dana settled down with the prize crossword, but her mind kept drifting back to Nicola's comments about Miss Latimer which had made her feel vaguely uncomfortable.

She and I will never be friends, she thought, but surely Adam can see she's just a silly, elderly woman. Besides she's right in one way. Adam does need a wife—and children.

That was an aspect she'd never contemplated before, she thought blankly. It had all been about winning. Getting what she wanted, rather than what might be required of her in return.

But she wouldn't worry too much. She didn't yearn to be a mother, but it was a natural consequence of marriage and she would deal with it when the time came.

But for now, she thought luxuriously, stretching out on her padded lounger, time could simply—slip by.

'Wake up, Sleeping Beauty.'

The words seemed to be part of the dream she'd been having. A bed, soft as a cloud, and someone's arms—Adam's arms—holding her close.

Smiling, she opened her eyes and found Adam—no longer a dream—bending over her.

'Heavens.' She struggled upright, pushing at her hair. 'Please tell me I wasn't snoring.'

'Not a sound,' he said. 'Scout's honour.'

'I bet you were never in the Scouts. Did you enjoy your golf?

'We didn't play. Zac apparently had other plans, so I spent some time on the driving range.' He paused. 'And you didn't fancy the castle ruins?'

'I've seen them before.'

'But not for quite a while.' Another silence. 'Do you ever think about those days—when you lived here?'

Think about them? *Think about them?*

Dana bit back a peal of hysterical laughter and shrugged. 'I don't tend to dwell in the past,' she lied. 'I prefer to look forward.'

He hitched a chair forward and sat beside her. 'I can't get over how different you are.'

'Well, I'm certainly not a schoolgirl any more.'

'I noticed,' he said. 'But there is—stuff that I remember from those days.' He looked awkward. 'Things, maybe, that shouldn't have happened.'

Her heart leapt. She kept her voice casual. 'It was a long time ago, and we've both changed. Perhaps we should agree to forget the past.'

The blue eyes looked into hers. He said slowly, 'I'm not so sure I want to forget—all of it.'

Hardly breathing, she waited for him to reach for her. Take her hand. Draw her towards him.

Only to see a shadow fall across the terrace.

'So here you are,' Zac drawled. 'How convenient. You can both enjoy this pleasant surprise.'

He turned to the tall blonde girl standing almost hesitantly in the French windows, a brief blue dress showing off an expensive tan.

'Robina, *cara*.' His voice was a caress. 'Come here and make Adam a happy man again.'

There was a silence that could have been cut with a knife. Adam rose slowly from his chair.

'Robina, sweetheart, where did you spring from?' He walked across the terrace to her side.

'Just the railway station.' She gave a little excited laugh. 'I rang Zac earlier and asked him to pick me up. Is it really a nice surprise?'

Move, said a voice in Dana's head as Robina's hands went up to Adam's shoulders and she offered her lips for his kiss. Move now. Stand up politely. Show nothing—no frustration, no disappointment—because you know you're being watched.

Her body felt stiff, unwilling to obey, but she lifted herself from the lounger, the newspaper sliding from her lap.

She watched them kiss, waiting for jealousy to rip into her—tear her apart, but all she actually felt was anger. And its focus was neither Adam nor the girl clinging to him, but Zac, quiet and observant beside her.

She said brightly, 'Adam, aren't you going to introduce us?'

'Of course.' Adam led Robina forward. 'Dana Grantham, meet Robina Simmons.'

'I'm an old friend of Adam's sister,' Dana said easily, encountering a faintly limp handshake. 'We've rather lost touch over the years, so this weekend has been catch-up time.'

Robina nodded. 'And Mannion is such a lovely place for it to happen. I always think it's a little corner of Paradise.'

Complete with serpent, thought Dana.

'Well,' Adam said breezily. 'Let's take your things upstairs, my sweet, and get you settled in.'

Plus another more private reunion, thought Dana as they disappeared into the house together, Robina chattering excitedly.

Zac broke the taut silence. 'Please understand that you are wasting your time.'

She had not expected quite such a blunt approach, and for a moment, it threw her.

But only for a moment.

'Why do you still begrudge me a pleasant weekend in the country?' she asked coolly. 'After all, I do work very hard.'

He nodded reflectively. 'Yes,' he said. 'That I grant you because I have been watching you do so. But you would have done better to stay away.'

'I am not here as your guest, Mr Belisandro.' Dana lifted her chin. 'Kindly remember that.'

He inclined his head with mocking courtesy. 'Believe me, *signorina*, it is a situation that I find it quite impossible to forget.'

His dark gaze suddenly seemed to blaze at her, not with anger, but something even more disturbing, his eyes travelling from her parted lips to the rounded swell of her breasts under the cling of her silky top. Reminding her how his hands and lips had once caressed her.

Mouth dry, Dana took a step away from him, her foot brushing against the newspaper and pen lying forgotten on the flagstones.

She bent to retrieve them but Zac got there first, glancing down at the unfinished crossword as he held it out to her.

He said, 'Fourteen down is "Azerbaijan".'

'You finish it,' she said, turning away. 'As you seem to think you have all the answers.' And went into the house.

Even with the window open, her room was like

an oven, but Dana was already boiling inwardly. She slammed the door and leaned against it, staring ahead of her with eyes that saw nothing.

Why was he doing this? she asked herself. He was the virtual ruler of a great multinational organisation with worldwide interests in mining, shipping, agriculture, technology and tourism. He was related to the Latimers only because his father and Serafina were first cousins.

So, where in this busy and exhausting life did he find time to interest himself in Adam's choice of wife?

It was like playing chess against a grand master, she thought. Finding your every move blocked with a mocking murmur of 'Check'. Feeling increasingly out of your depth. Being driven inexorably to the moment when you'd overturn your piece in defeat.

And, right now, she was tempted to do exactly that. To invent some emergency and leave. Concentrate her energies on her career. Perhaps find contentment in a new relationship.

Except…

What peace of mind could she hope for if she allowed herself to be—mugged like this? To meekly give up Mannion without a fight—something that she wanted more than anything in the world, and that, morally and emotionally, already belonged to her?

Leaving her to wonder 'what if' for the rest of her life?

Robina's arrival was a setback, nothing more. It was Adam who would ultimately shape his own future. And she had to make sure that she, and no one else, was part of that.

Starting tonight.

'Aunt Mimi is like a dog with two tails,' Nicola said wrathfully. She and Dana had gone for a stroll in the garden, filling in the time before they needed to change for the party.

'She's telling everyone she knew it was just a lovers' tiff and that reason would prevail in the end. She even suggested to my future mother-in-law that when Adam proposed the toast to Eddie and me this evening, he should announce his own engagement at the same time.'

'Oh, God.' Dana bit her lip. 'What did she say?'

Nicola grinned. 'She began with "Over my dead body" and went on from there, adding pretty forcefully that Adam's life is his own business.'

She paused. 'What I can't figure is how Zac got involved. Unless he fancies Robina for himself. Since his father's heart problems, he must be under real pressure to marry.'

'Poor Robina,' Dana said lightly, aware of a sudden inner jolt.

'You must be joking. When Zac eventually picks a wife, the world will be filled with the noise of shattered female hearts. And not just because he's mega rich,' she added drily. 'Rumour has it that he's a tiger in the bedroom.'

'But who believes rumours?' said Dana, lifting a hand ostensibly to push her hair back from her face, but actually to conceal that she was blushing. Aware too that she was trembling inside.

Which I don't need, even if it's with rage, she told herself grimly as they went back to the house.

Later, studying herself in the bathroom mirror, she felt moderately satisfied with the result. Tonight, she'd gone for basic black, a slender ankle-length sheath, cut high to the throat, but swooping wickedly at the back. Her newly washed hair was swept up into a loose knot on top of her head, with a few tendrils allowed to escape and frame her face, without concealing the jet hoops in her ears. Her eyes expertly shadowed looked exotic and mysterious, while her mouth, by contrast, was all innocence, painted a delicate pale rose.

Sophisticated? Maybe. Alluring? Perhaps. Enough to catch Adam's attention and keep it? In the lap of the gods. But it would not be for want of trying.

She waited deliberately until the last minute before going down to the drawing room, aiming to time her entry so that she'd be the last to appear. But she hadn't allowed for Robina's famous unpunctuality, as one glance told her that she and Adam were still missing.

Damn, she thought, laughing and bobbing a mock curtsy in response to Eddie's cheerfully non-PC wolf whistle. And avoiding even a glance in Zac's direction.

She'd spotted him, lean and elegant in dinner jacket and black tie as soon as she'd walked in, that one fleeting look inflicting a potent reminder of the last time she'd seen him in evening clothes. The cool magic of his mouth in the darkness. The brooding gaze absorbing her half-naked body in the candlelight.

All of it telling her remorselessly that she was still a long way from forgetting.

Swiftly, she joined Emily and the others, laughing and chatting as if she didn't have a care in the world.

The room soon began to fill up, with groups spilling out on to the terrace and the lawns beneath, so it was easy to lose herself among them.

Waitresses, hired for the occasion, carried round trays of wine and soft drinks, and a pianist provided a muted background of popular music old and new.

In the middle of it all, Adam walked in tight-lipped, in marked contrast to Robina who was smiling radiantly beside him in a white dress with a tiered lace skirt and white flowers in her hair.

'Dear child.' Aunt Mimi's voice rang out effusively above the buzz of conversation, bringing it to a virtual halt. 'How lovely you look. Just like a bride.'

Oh, God, thought Dana watching Nicola and Eddie exchange resigned looks. The woman must have a death wish. And I suppose I should be grateful to her, judging by Adam's expression. Yet, somehow, I'm not.

She wandered on to the terrace and chose some chicken salad from the buffet, more for the sake of having something to do than because she was hungry.

And it was here that Adam found her later, leaning against the stone balustrade and sipping a glass of Sauvignon Blanc as she watched half a dozen couples at the other end of the terrace moving slowly in the twilight to the music wafting from the drawing room.

He said quietly, 'I've had about enough of this party. What the hell was Nic thinking of? I can't wait to propose the toast and watch them all leave.'

'Well, you'll have to get used to it,' she returned lightly, wondering where he'd left Robina. 'Mannion was made for entertaining, and as Nic's having her wedding reception here, think how many toasts that will involve.'

He grimaced. 'I'll cross that bridge if and when I come to it.' He paused. 'Dana, we need to talk, but it's hopeless here, like living in a spotlight.

Can I call you at work next week? Fix something up? Drinks, maybe, or dinner?'

She studied her wine, quelling the bubble of triumph within her. 'Do you think you should?'

'Why not? You're a free agent, I presume.'

'But you,' she said, 'are not. And I don't want to cause a rift between you and Robina.'

He said with faint grimness, 'You won't. She's a lovely girl and we've had fun, but it's over. We want different things.'

Does she know that? Dana wondered with a touch of unease. However, that is not my problem.

Adam moved nearer. His voice dropped another level. 'Do you know how bloody fantastic you look tonight?'

'You mean the plan has actually worked? Or do I say—what, in this old thing?'

'You knock every other woman in the room sideways,' he said slowly. 'I should have seen it years ago.'

But I thought you did...

For an instant she was jarred, but dismissed it as a niggle. Because the past didn't matter when there was the here and now. And the promise of the future.

The familiar strains of 'As Time Goes By' came floating through the gathering darkness. Adam took the glass from her hand and set it on the balustrade.

He said, smiling, 'I think he's playing our tune. Come and dance with me.'

Dana went into his arms, feeling as if time had actually rolled back. That this was how it should have been seven years ago. But worth waiting for, she thought feeling the warmth of his hand on her bare back as they began to move slowly to the music.

She'd imagined this moment so many times. Known exactly how she wanted it to be. Dreamed of her response, skin, bone and blood, to his touch.

Yet the reality was different. Paramount was a kind of satisfaction at being held in Adam's arms for all to see. And her emotional and sensual re-action would impact later when her hopes became certainties. All she needed was time. And privacy.

She closed her eyes, listening to the melody,

trying to capture the right mood, only to be interrupted by Zac's voice, coolly amused and much too close at hand.

'It is time for the toast, my dear Adam, or do you wish me to act as your substitute?'

'No, of course I'll do it.' Adam glanced round at the other pairs, still entwined, and raised his voice. 'Back inside, everyone and let's drink to the happy couple.'

As the terrace began to clear, Dana deliberately hung back, and was glad she'd done so when she saw Robina move to Adam's side, sliding a possessive hand through his arm.

She felt a pang—not jealousy or even remorse. Perhaps it was sympathy mixed with relief that she was not responsible for the heartache heading Robina's way. That Adam's decision had been made when the weekend began.

He was in his element, very much the master of the house as he made his brief speech, his words warm, affectionate and amusing.

I wonder who'll do this for us when we're engaged, Dana thought as she raised her glass amid the laughter and applause. Perhaps Eddie.

Certainly there'd be no good wishes for her

future with Adam coming from Zac, who was leaning in the drawing room doorway, his dark face expressionless.

Well, let him think what he wants, she thought biting her lip. Let him discover that he can't win them all. It will be good for his soul if not his temper.

She set herself to enjoy the rest of the party, dancing with anyone who asked her, chatting to the older couples who remembered her kindly and explaining a dozen tines how she and Nicola had chanced to meet again. Resigned to the knowledge that she would spend no more time with Adam that evening, with Robina apparently glued to his side.

Her face had begun to ache with smiling, her body tense with the effort of trying to be wherever Zac was not, so it was a relief when people started to go and she could relax a little.

There would be coffee and sandwiches in the drawing room for the house guests, but Dana decided to slip away to her room and made a quiet excuse to Nicola.

She paused in the dark hall, drawing a deep breath as she looked up at the unlit chandelier, remembering how Adam had once caught her here and kissed her.

From behind her Zac said softly, 'Sadly, it is the wrong time of year for mistletoe, *mia bella*, so you must console yourself with memories.'

She spun round gasping to meet the mockery in his eyes.

'You were spying on us?' Her voice rose.

He shrugged. 'I was merely coming downstairs. Adam knew, but you, *mia cara*, were too absorbed in your Christmas idyll to notice me.'

She said curtly, 'I was a child.'

'A child,' he said, 'learning to be a woman, as we both have cause to remember.'

But I don't want to remember, she thought. I want to forget everything you've ever said or done to me, as if it never happened. Just as I don't want to be here in the dark with you now.

Her voice shook. 'I'm not in a reminiscent mood. Excuse me, please.'

She turned to head for the stairs, but Zac halted her, his hands lightly clasping her hips, drawing her back against him.

He said quietly, 'Not yet.'

They were not alone. She could hear, as he

must, the voices from the dining room, a mere stone's throw away.

All she had to do was call out and someone would come.

She felt his lips gently brush the nape of her neck, then continue slowly downwards between her shoulder blades, his kisses delineating every bone in her spine with tantalising delicacy.

She heard herself gasp. Felt the sharp inner clench of her body—the sudden heaviness of her breasts as their tumescent nipples pressed against the concealment of her dress in potent self-betrayal.

Wrong, she thought feverishly. This is so wrong.

Although this was exactly why she was wearing this elegant tease of a dress. But it was Adam who should have been here with her, ready to fulfil the vivid desires of her imagination,

Adam whom she wanted to turn her in his arms and kiss her mouth, then untie the knot of her halter-neck and take her swollen, aching breasts in his hands.

Adam—to carry her upstairs to his room and lie between her thighs on a soft, cool bed.

Not this other—her nemesis, who had harmed

her enough already. Who had to be stopped before this went any further.

'Let me go.' The words might be hers, but the voice, driven and husky, belonged to a stranger. 'Let me go—now.'

For a moment, he did nothing. Simply stood, his warm breath stirring the loose tendrils of hair on the back of her neck. Then, as her own breathing quickened in what she told herself was panic, he lifted his hands from her hips and she was free.

Free to cross to the stairs. To climb to the place where they curved and pause, for some incomprehensible reason, to look back over her shoulder.

Only to find the hall below silent and empty.

Which in some curious way, was also how she felt.

'Madness,' she whispered under her breath. Total madness. And she went on up the stairs into yet more darkness.

CHAPTER SEVEN

ONLY NICOLA AND Eddie were in the dining room when she went down to breakfast the following morning.

'Where is everyone?' she queried, taking a seat.

'Mum and Dad have gone to church to have another word with the Vicar, and the gang are playing tennis before it gets too hot.' Eddie was heaping marmalade onto his toast.

'Like my parents, you were wise to disappear last night,' he added. 'Because, not long afterwards, all hell broke loose over the bedtime snacks when Nic's aunt Mimi, who must have been a pit bull in an earlier life, went back to the subject of Adam's marital prospects.'

He shook his head. 'Consequently, Zac is driving a tear-stained Robina back to London to clear her stuff from Adam's flat, and he's following them, presumably to make sure she doesn't miss anything.'

'While Aunt Mimi has taken to her bed with some eau de cologne and a bottle of aspirin,' added Nicola, handing Dana her coffee. 'Hurrah for a weekend in the country.'

'Oh,' Dana said slowly. 'Oh, dear.'

'My sentiments entirely,' said Eddie. He studied her, frowning. 'But I have to say you look as if you could use some aspirin and eau de cologne yourself.'

A good night's sleep was all she really needed, thought Dana. And to wake to good news.

Zac's absence was naturally a relief, but she'd counted on seeing Adam today to make some definite arrangements for their next meeting. His departure without a word was an unexpected setback.

She smiled with an effort. 'Self-inflicted wound caused by too much champagne. I'll recover.'

She paused. 'I'm sorry about Robina. But it might teach Mr Belisandro to think twice before interfering in Adam's private life.'

'Apparently that was all her own idea,' said Nicola. 'She sent Zac a text asking him to meet her, then just got on the train and came. He told her it was a mistake and urged her to go back to London, but she wouldn't listen.'

Dana made an effort to speak lightly. 'Perhaps he'll console her, as you suggested, by offering her the vacant post of Mrs Belisandro.'

Eddie gave her an old-fashioned look. 'That,' he said, 'I doubt very much.'

It was a long morning and Dana soon regretted her decision to leave after lunch with the rest of the group. Mimi Latimer appeared at coffee time, clutching a handkerchief with the melancholy air of Joan of Arc at the stake.

She really sees herself as the injured party in all this, Dana thought fascinated, as she observed the Marchwoods' unavailing efforts to divert her into a more cheerful frame of mind.

She finished her coffee quickly, and went up to pack, finding Mrs Harris coming out of her room.

'I was asked to give you a note, Miss Grantham. It's been rather hectic this morning so I've left it on your night table.'

'Oh, thank you.' Dana affected an air of nonchalance to hide the fact that her heart was beating nineteen to the dozen.

An envelope was propped against the bedside lamp, containing a single sheet of notepaper. And a four word message, with no signature.

'Until we meet again.'

So Adam did think of me after all, Dana told herself exultantly.

'Until we meet again,' she whispered, crushing the note in her hand. 'And it can't be soon enough for me.'

However ten days passed before the receptionist at Jarvis Stratton told her there was a personal call for her on line two, and even then she thought it was probably Nicola.

Instead: 'Hi,' said Adam. 'How's the property market?'

At last, thought Dana, suppressing a sigh of relief. She kept her tone casual. 'In good nick, thanks. How's the world of public relations?'

'Just now I'm more interested in the private kind. Can I persuade you to join me for lunch today?'

Dana hesitated. He was taking a lot for granted. Anyone else and she'd have invented a prior engagement, and suggested the following week.

But why take the risk, just for the sake of her pride?

'You called at the right moment,' she said. 'I was just going to order a sandwich.'

'Great. There's a wine bar not far from you called Sam's Place. Why don't we meet there at one?'

'Why not indeed,' she said, adding, 'Must go. There's a call on another line.'

It wasn't true, but she was afraid of letting her inner jubilation show.

She wished she'd picked something more interesting to wear than a navy skirt and a blue-and-white-striped blouse. But what could he expect in the middle of a working day? she asked herself, as she freshened her lipstick and applied a discreet misting of scent to her wrists and throat.

Adam was waiting at the bar when she walked in.

'It's busy,' she said, glancing around her.

'Always, but I've got us a table in the courtyard at the back, and a bottle of Frascati on ice.'

'One of my favourites,' said Dana, mentally resolving to restrict herself to a single glass.

'Hardly the way to celebrate our proper reunion,' Adam commented when they'd sat down and ordered their food. 'But I didn't want to wait any longer.'

Then why did you?

'And I didn't have your mobile number,' he went on. 'I should have asked at Mannion, only the situation became rather fraught.'

Or you could have asked Nicola…

'I guess that's now settled.' She made herself sound matter of fact, and he sighed.

'Yes, thank Heaven,' he said, adding swiftly, 'which is no reflection on Robina. She's a wonderful girl and one day she'll make some fortunate man very happy. Only it was never going to be me.'

It was the kind of assurance she wanted from him, so why did she still feel so edgy?

The arrival of a basket of crusty bread and a bowl of olives made things slightly easier.

Searching for a neutral topic, she said, 'Do you still play tennis?'

'Hardly ever. My interests are sea-based these days. I belong to a sailing club on the south coast, and I do a lot of surfing and scuba diving in

Cornwall and other places. I also belong to a club that looks for wrecks.'

'Sunken treasure?'

He laughed. 'Some hopes. But the ocean still remains the planet's greatest undiscovered wilderness and it fascinates me. Nic, of course, thinks I'm nuts,' he added. 'But she's not very adventurous. Her dream is a home and babies with Eddie.'

It was almost a sneer and it disturbed her.

She said lightly, 'Well, that's what keeps the world turning while the men are off in the wilderness.'

'It's probably why they go.'

Ouch, thought Dana, wincing inwardly. I walked into that.

Adam leaned forward. 'Look, Dana, I won't pretend life's been ideal in recent years. Frankly, I've been inclined to drift in a number of ways, but that's all changing now. I have an aim in life. A purpose that wasn't there before. Can you understand that?'

Yes, thought Dana. The legal situation over the house has left you in a kind of limbo, but that's ending soon, and Mannion will be yours at last.

Aloud, she said, 'Of course. None better.'

'Then there's no need for awkward questions—on either side. We're both adults and know how things can be.'

He means his love life, thought Dana, and he was clearly crediting her with a level of sophistication she did not possess. She was glad when his steak and chips and her Caesar salad were delivered.

The food was good, but Dana declined a dessert and put a firm hand over her glass when Adam tried to refill it.

'I have to work this afternoon,' she told him. 'We both do.'

'Ah,' he said. 'And I was hoping to persuade you to play truant on this lovely afternoon. Enjoy the wine here and maybe open another bottle at my flat.' He reached across the table, his fingers stroking hers. 'It's only a short cab ride away and I'm sure we could both find adequate excuses for being absent from our desks.'

'You perhaps,' said Dana. 'But I have appointments which I cannot miss.' She paused, her smile regretful. 'However tempting the offer.'

'You really want to spend the rest of your life doing upmarket property deals?'

'Not entirely,' she said. 'But, for now, it pays well and I like it. Two good reasons for hanging in there.'

'Whereas I can't wait to make a complete break and move on.' Adam spoke with sudden harsh intensity. 'Be my own boss again, instead of existing at Zac's beck and call.'

'You mean when Serafina—Mrs Latimer—finally hands over Mannion.'

'Yes,' he said. 'I can hardly wait.'

And nor, thought Dana, can I.

He paused. 'So I really can't persuade you to jump ship for a few hours.'

'Not this time.' She lowered her eyes demurely. 'I just have—too much to lose.'

'Then, when the time comes,' he said softly, 'I'll have to make sure it's worth it.'

I'm a foregone conclusion, thought Dana, observing his satisfied air as he asked for the bill, and irked by it.

As she had been by his assumption that she would agree to the wine and sex on offer at his flat.

However, he wouldn't find she was the easy

conquest he was probably accustomed to, she decided as she scribbled her mobile number on the back of a business card.

He merely kissed her cheek in parting, but the smouldering look he gave her, combined with the caress of his thumb against the palm of her hand, was anything but chaste.

All in all, she had a lot to think about as she walked back to the office.

It seemed she wasn't the only one who'd changed, and it occurred to her that if she and Adam had been meeting for the first time, she might well have concluded they had very little in common.

But that was negative thinking. They simply had to get to know each other all over again, that was all.

Besides, the way he'd spoken suggested that he'd sown his wild oats and was looking to settle down, and as that was what she wanted to hear, maybe she should scrub today's events and hope for better in future.

One encouraging aspect was Adam's clear desire to cut free from Belisandro International in general and Zac in particular.

And he can expect my full support on both counts, she told herself stormily, her footsteps quickening along with the beat of her heart.

'You and Adam?' Nicola was wide-eyed. 'When did this begin?'

'A fortnight ago.' Dana paused. 'He hasn't mentioned it?'

'I guessed there was someone,' Nicola admitted. 'Because there always is.' She gave Dana an anxious look. 'You do realise that, don't you?'

'We're keeping it casual,' Dana assured her.

Or I am, at least, she thought wryly. Because she was being subjected to constant pressure from Adam to allow their relationship to move to intimacy. And though he was undoubtedly intrigued by her equally constant resistance, she could sense that it was beginning to irritate him too.

But she had no intention of changing her mind—not until he gave her some real evidence of commitment.

And maybe his invitation to accompany him to the Belisandro International party the following week was a hopeful sign, while the news that

Nicola and Eddie were also to be guests was a definite bonus.

She'd known the Belisandro Pan-European conference was being held in London, because Adam had been complaining about the extra work involved, and the aggravating attention to detail that Zac required.

'All the male delegates' wives and girlfriends are receiving bracelets, and the women's partners get cufflinks—gold, of course,' he'd informed her. 'To be presented at the party by Signor Ottaviano, Big Daddy himself, back in full fighting trim after his op.' He snorted. 'Let's see how Wonder Boy likes playing second fiddle again.'

To her surprise, Dana had found herself wincing at his comments. After all, his own company had gone bust, and while he might only be a cog in the Belisandro PR machine, he'd walked into a job with a salary sufficient to support a frankly lavish lifestyle. Which he now seemed poised to jettison.

Presumably he'd been head-hunted for a position that would lift him into the millionaire bracket, so at least there'd be funds to restore Mannion to past glories.

'And wear that black thing you had for Nic's engagement party,' he'd added. 'I want to show you off.'

'Not possible, I'm afraid,' she returned coolly. 'I had it cleaned and sent it to a charity shop.'

'What the hell for?' He frowned. 'You looked stunning in it.'

She shrugged. 'It was a one occasion dress. Now it's someone else's turn to stun.'

And she could never have worn it again. Not when it would remind her of the brush of a man's mouth against her bared skin. The wrong man...

Besides, at this party, she did not want to attract attention—especially from the wrong man. And if she could have come up with a valid excuse, she would not be going at all.

She decided to stick to basic black, finding in a boutique a silky crepe dress with a demurely scooped neck, elbow-length sleeves and mid-calf skirt, so far from making a statement that it was positively reticent.

Adam, of course, told her that she looked gorgeous, a ritual that she suspected would be maintained even if she had a bag over her head.

They shared a cab with Nicola and Eddie to

the Hotel Capital Imperiale where the conference had been taking place. The party was in the first-floor ballroom, reached by a wide marble staircase and lit by opulent chandeliers, with music supplied by a jazz quartet from a corner rostrum.

'The food's in the next room,' said Adam. 'Mass catering on the grand scale.'

His derisory tone earned him a sharp look from his sister as she took a glass of champagne from the tray proffered by a hovering waiter.

'Good,' she said. 'Because I've been dieting all week to get into this blasted frock, and now I could eat a roasted ox—whole.'

Eddie slid an arm round her waist. 'Let's see if we can find one,' he began but was interrupted by a tall thin girl with glasses who came darting out of the crowd.

'Adam—at last. We have a problem.'

Adam detached his sleeve from her grasp. 'Carol, this is a party. Can't whatever it is wait until tomorrow?'

'No,' she said. 'Because it's about tonight. The gifts for the WAGs haven't been delivered and Signor Belisandro is expecting to make the presentation. It's one of the reasons he came over from Italy. Tell me that you did confirm time and date with the suppliers?'

Adam's mouth tightened. 'Yes, of course.' He added coldly, 'Do you want to check?'

'We'll have to. The hotel manager's arranged a room and a computer so we can find out what's gone wrong. Until we do, the party's over for both of us.'

Adam swore under his breath, then turned to Dana. 'My sweet, I'm really sorry. Stick with Nic and Eddie for half an hour while I look into this foul-up—if there is one.'

She forced a smile. 'Of course.' And added, 'Good luck.'

'He'll need it,' Nicola said caustically as he disappeared with Carol. 'If I'm any judge, it'll take more than half an hour and a lot of fast talking to get out of this one.'

Dana stared at her. 'You think it's his fault?'

'I'd put money on it. Adam prefers the big picture, the grand gesture. He sees details like delivery dates to be the province of lesser mortals. Which is probably why Carol got promoted and he didn't.'

It also explains why he's so keen to change

jobs, thought Dana as they made their way to the buffet.

Nicola gave a sigh of bliss when she saw the carvery offering sizzling hot joints of beef, ham and turkey on one side of the room, and the cold table on the other, with every kind of seafood and a mouthwatering display of exotic salads.

Her companions tucked into the meat with gusto, while Dana, beginning to wish herself a hundred miles away, confined herself to a modest helping of lobster and rice.

Nicola's prediction proved to be correct, and over an hour went by with no sign of Adam. And being without him was making her feel oddly vulnerable.

'I think I'll just slip away,' she told her companions, remaining firm in the face of their protests.

She was crossing the huge foyer to the cloakroom to find her wrap, when she heard her name. She turned to see Zac emerging from a lift and paused reluctantly.

As he reached her, he said, 'I hope you are not leaving.'

'Yes, I am. When Adam invited me here tonight, he was not expecting to spend the evening working.'

'I regret your mutual disappointment, but if he had carried out the task assigned to him, it would not have happened,' he said. 'Also your invitation came from me. If you remember, I promised we would meet again.'

She stared at him. 'You—promised?'

'In my note,' he said. 'You did receive it?'

'Yes,' she said thickly. 'But I didn't realise it was from you.'

'Ah,' he said lightly. 'Another disappointment. But you cannot go yet. There is someone who wishes to meet you.'

'Thank you,' she said. 'However, if you don't mind, I'll stick to my original plan and find a cab.'

'But I do mind, Dana *mia*.' He took her hand. 'Because I wish you to stay. Besides, my father does not care to be kept waiting.'

His father…

'That's unfortunate.' She tried unavailingly to free herself.

'Or for having his wishes thwarted.'

She glared at him. 'It must run in the family.'

His grin mocked her. 'I congratulate you on your perception, *mia bella*.'

'And I am not beautiful,' she snapped back.

'Not perhaps in that dull dress,' Zac agreed softly. 'But without it—*Madonna*!'

To her fury, Dana found she was not only speechless but blushing to the roots of her hair as she was conducted into the lift, and carried swiftly and silently straight up to the top floor.

CHAPTER EIGHT

HER IMMEDIATE THOUGHT was that if she had merely seen Ottaviano Belisandro in the street, she would have known instantly whose father he was.

Her second, that she could also see with total clarity how Zac himself would look at that age, his dark hair silvery grey, the lines of his face more deeply incised, but still a man to be reckoned with, his vigour undiminished. And wondered how she could be so sure. Or why it should matter.

She was surprised to find no entourage gathered in the room. No telephones ringing, no buzz of conversation or hum of technology.

But the fact that he was alone as he rose to greet her emphasised, in some contradictory way, the aura of effortless power which surrounded him. And which he had passed on to his son.

'Papà,' Zac said. 'Allow me to introduce Miss Dana Grantham.'

'This is a pleasure for me.' His voice was more heavily accented than his son's. His handshake was firm and his gaze frankly searching as he waved her to the chair on the other side of an ornate marble fireplace. 'Please to sit, *signorina*.'

Dana obeyed reluctantly, conscious that Zac had stationed himself behind her, his hand on the back of her chair. Near enough to touch, but not doing so, she realised, her body tensing in nervous awareness.

'I am glad to meet at last the niece of the lady who cares for my cousin Serafina with such kindness and devotion.' Ottaviano Belisandro resumed his seat. 'I regret that it has not happened before. But you have never visited your aunt in Italy, *signorina*. Why is that?'

The truthful reply to a question she'd not expected would be, 'Because I wouldn't be welcome.' So she tried polite evasion. 'I have a demanding job, Signor Belisandro. My holidays tend to be last minute and confined to this country.'

'Then you are missing a delight, *signorina*. My cousin Serafina lives very near me on the shore of Lake Como, one of the most beautiful places in the world, as you should see for yourself.'

He paused. 'It means much to you, this work of yours?'

Yes, of course...

Again, the words hovered unspoken on her lips. Because career satisfaction wasn't her goal and never had been. It was Mannion that mattered. It was everything to her. All she would ever care about, with no room in her life for anything—or anyone—else.

Something she wanted to shout aloud for the whole of London to hear, and, in particular, the man standing close behind her. Too close.

She needed to break the silence that seemed to be closing around her. The strange weakness that was making her tremble inside. The feeling that she was spinning into chaos. Into delusion.

Oh, God, she thought. What's happening to me? What am I thinking? Why am I here instead of downstairs with Adam? Except he's trapped in a meeting and I—I'm trapped here.

Her voice seemed to come from some immense distance. 'Jarvis Stratton is one of London's premier property agencies. It's a privilege to work there, so I feel very fortunate.'

The truth, the whole truth and nothing but the truth. Somewhere convenient to hide from doubt, fear and damaging admissions.

'Fortunate indeed,' agreed her inquisitor. 'But for a young and beautiful woman there must be more. For you, *signorina*, are there no dreams?'

She summoned a smile from somewhere. Spoke lightly. 'In today's economic climate, Signor Belisandro, dreams are an expensive luxury that not all of us can afford.'

She rose. 'Thank you for receiving me so graciously, but I've taken up quite enough of your time. I should rejoin my friends.'

He stood up too. 'Then my son will escort you and when I have made one phone call, I too shall come down and join the party. We will all drink a glass of wine together, no?'

No...

The word echoed crazily in her brain, just as it had done that afternoon when she'd seen Zac waiting on the terrace—like a dark cloud on her horizon.

A dark cloud fast becoming a storm that might

sweep her away if she didn't fight it. Fight for the life she had chosen.

She tried another bland, meaningless smile. 'How kind of you, *signor*. But so many other people will be waiting to talk to you and to—to your son. I should be in the way. Good evening.'

Somehow, she got herself out of the room and across the corridor to the lift, with Zac, she realised, one step behind her.

As she reached for the button, his hand closed over hers. 'Are you so determined to run away?'

'I was trying to leave earlier when you stopped me.' She stared at the lift doors, willing them to open of their own volition. To open and save her.

'And now I am asking you to stay.'

'To drink wine with your father?' Her voice sounded breathless as if she was a nervous schoolgirl again. 'Is that what he should be doing after a heart operation?'

'No,' he said. 'To both your questions. But that does not change what I am asking, so do not pretend not to understand me. Because you know, *mia bella*, that I want you to stay until the party ends, and to be with me tonight.'

'Then my answer is also no,' she said, staring

down at the crimson carpet, then at the wall. Anywhere that she could escape the way he was looking at her. Escape the memory of his mouth and the shameful, incomprehensible weakness that his lightest touch could evoke in her treacherous flesh.

She swallowed. 'And how dare you insult me like that when you know—you must know perfectly well that I belong to Adam.'

'Another pretence,' he said. 'Because you have never yet belonged to anyone. Nor are you sure enough of Adam to give yourself to him. In this, at least, you are wise.'

She did look at him then—glaring. 'I hardly think you, of all people, should lecture me on morality.'

'I do not speak of morals,' he said calmly. 'Only common sense.'

'And mine,' she said, 'is telling me to walk out right now. Unless you mean to keep me here by force.'

'I would not need to use force,' Zac said quietly. 'As you, my sweet hypocrite, know—perfectly well.' He paused. 'Or do you wish me to prove it?'

She said in a suffocated voice, 'All I want is to get away from you and your vile insinuations— for ever.'

Zac released her hand, pressed the button on the panel and stood back as the lift doors slid open.

'*Buona notte,* Dana *mia.*' His tone was unruffled. 'Sleep well.'

She walked into the lift and looked back at him, her chin raised defiantly. 'Aren't you going to wish me sweet dreams?'

'By no means.' His slow smile sent a quiver along her nerve endings. 'Because, if you stayed, you would find reality even sweeter.'

And it was that smile which remained with her, haunted her, all the way back to the safety of her flat.

'All right, I made a mistake. I admit it.' Adam shrugged. 'But it wasn't a disaster. The presentation was a day late, that's all. And there was no need for that blasted Carol to keep banging on about it until two a.m.' He snorted. 'I suppose she's worried about her job.'

Dana gave him a careful look. 'You don't have the same concerns?'

'I might,' he said. 'If I cared about the job-for-life pension scheme and paid-sick-leave existence. But I have other plans.'

And when, thought Dana, are you going to tell me what they are? Because I really need to know—to invest in our future. To get my own plans back on track where they belong, without unnecessary and destructive diversions.

'But at least,' Adam went on, 'the great Don Ottaviano goes back to Italy tomorrow, so we can all stop jumping at our own shadows.'

Dana frowned. 'You make him sound like a Mafia boss,' she protested.

He shrugged. 'Maybe that's how he comes across—only dealing in people's livelihoods instead of lives. Apparently he put in a formal appearance at the party, and everyone had to go up and pay homage, Nic and Eddie among them. At least you missed that.'

'Yes.' Dana forced a smile. 'Lucky me.'

'And no sooner does one Belisandro go but another arrives,' he added with faint irritation. 'Although Serafina is at least coming over for my benefit, so I shouldn't complain.'

No, thought Dana. You shouldn't.

'Is my aunt accompanying her?'

'It's a flying visit. She's coming alone—although, of course, she'll have Zac as her shield and protector when she gets here.'

Dana was disappointed, but hid it by making a business of looking at her watch. 'Well, I must dash. I have an accompanied viewing booked and my car's on a meter.'

'There's always something,' Adam objected moodily. 'For God's sake, Dana, when are we going to get together—I mean *really* together?'

She hesitated. 'When the time is right,' she said. 'At the moment we both have other things on our minds.'

And was glad she did not have to spell out her own preoccupations.

Because Adam had not been the only one still awake at 2:00 a.m. on the night of the party, staring blindly into the darkness and wondering if it would take a frontal lobotomy to finally rid herself of Zac Belisandro.

And telling herself she was being a complete fool was no help at all.

Yet what was the big problem? she asked herself defensively as she headed for her appointment. Zac had propositioned her. She'd turned him down.

He probably didn't get many rejections but— what the hell?—he'd get over it like other men whose paths had crossed hers. End of story.

And she would spend no more time battling with demons who had no right to exist. No right—and, more importantly, no reason.

Of course she was doing the right thing, Dana told herself as she drove down to Mannion.

She'd held Adam off quite long enough. Now, on his big day when, after seven years, he'd finally taken possession of his house, she would give him further cause to celebrate by joining him there.

She was thankful it was all over. Adam had been undeniably difficult in the past few days, edgy and even morose at times, and, at others, determinedly almost aggressively amorous. It had required all her persuasive powers to keep him at a safe distance for a while longer.

But her resistance seemed to have paid off, because when she'd last seen him two evenings ago, he'd whispered, 'When this Mannion business is completed, you and I are due for a serious talk.'

That, she thought, with a light jolt, suggested a proposal. A tad premature, maybe, but exactly what she'd been working towards, so she could hardly quibble. And Mannion would make the perfect setting for such a moment.

At first, she'd intended her arrival to be a complete surprise, but decided it was better to be cautious in case Serafina had opted to stay on for some reason instead of returning immediately to Italy.

Adam's mobile seemed to be switched off, so she'd called the house, only to get the answering machine.

'I've been thinking,' she said. 'Why don't I bring down some champagne and an overnight case and congratulate you in person? If it's a problem, let me know. I'll be leaving around three p.m.'

She'd anticipated a call or a text, telling her he

could hardly wait, but there was nothing. However, after a brief mental tussle, she decided to go anyway. After all, she'd booked out a day's leave from work, and spent the morning in the beauty salon being waxed, massaged and toned, and having her finger and toenails painted in a soft coral to match her new dress.

She was naturally nervous at the prospect of practically presenting herself to him, gift-wrapped, but told herself not to be silly. Didn't they say, 'Who dares, wins.'

Well, yes, but they, whoever they were, also claimed that 'the end justified the means', which was not so appealing but probably nearer the truth. And the fact was, she needed some Dutch courage to aid her victory.

She'd hoped Adam would answer the door, but instead was confronted by a faintly surprised Mrs Harris.

'Miss Grantham?' she said, giving Dana's overnight case a surprised glance.

Dana produced a confident smile. 'The new master of the house,' she said. 'He is here?'

'Well, yes.' The older woman paused. 'If you'll

wait in the book room, miss, I'll tell him you
wish to speak to him.'

More than speak, thought Dana, banishing the
doubts quivering within her like butterflies as she
followed the housekeeper. I intend to kiss him,
drink a bottle of Cristal with him and, eventually, go to bed with him. No turning back now.

In the book room, she took the champagne
from her case and placed it on the desk, turning
with a smile as she heard someone enter.

'*Buongiorno,* Dana *mia.*' Zac closed the door
behind him and strolled forward. 'And welcome.'

'You,' she said hoarsely. 'What the hell are you
doing here? And where's Adam?'

'By now in London. He returned there after
driving Serafina to the airport. He wished, naturally, to thank her for her past kindness and say
a final *addio.*'

'Final?' Dana repeated. 'Is she ill?'

'She is about to undergo a hip operation but
Adam's goodbye was necessary because he is
unlikely to meet with her again in the foresee-
able future. He will be far too busy in Australia.'
He paused. 'Or has he not discussed his plans
with you?'

She stared at him, his words beating a tattoo in her skull. One word in particular. *Australia*...

She said unevenly, 'I suppose this is your doing. That you're sending him to work in Melbourne.'

'I respect my colleagues there too much to inflict Adam upon them.' His tone was curt. 'No, he is buying a partnership in the boat chartering business on the Gold Coast owned by his father and uncle by marriage. He leaves next week.'

She was leaning back against the desk, her hands gripping its edge so tightly that the oak bit into her palms.

She said, 'After waiting all this time for Mannion, he's throwing it away to go to Australia of all places? I don't believe it.'

'Why not?' Zac's shrug was negligent. 'His father walked away. His mother too, for that matter.'

'But he can't just abandon it. If this move to Australia doesn't work out, he'll need Mannion to come back to.'

His mouth twisted. 'On the contrary, *mia bella*, I think he abandoned it a long time ago, as you must have seen for yourself.'

'Then why did he agree to the gift in the first place?'

He said quietly, 'Serafina is an honourable woman who wished her husband's home to remain with the Latimers but unburdened by extra taxation. When his father decided he preferred a life in the sun, Adam became the heir.

'In the beginning, he was flattered. But it was not long before he began to think of the financial benefit it could bring him.'

'You mean he's planning to rent it out while he's away?' Dana asked with sudden eagerness.

'No,' Zac said. 'That is not what I mean.'

'Well, he can't leave it empty, so he'll have to put in caretakers.' She began to smile. 'Which is perfect, because whatever he's paying them, I'll do it for less—and do it better. That's an offer he can't refuse.'

'And the job in London you do so well?' Zac countered silkily. 'What of that?'

'You don't get it, do you?' she blazed at him. 'You don't see that the only thing that counts— that's ever mattered to me—is Mannion. That I've wanted it all my life and that I'd do any-thing—make any sacrifice—to live here again.

To look after it and bring it back to the way it used to be.'

'You are wrong, *mia bella*,' he said with a touch of grimness. 'I have always known these things. Why else would we be having this conversation?'

She was barely listening. 'I must get back to London. Talk to him.'

'You would be wasting your time.'

'You can't say that,' she returned defiantly. 'He'll be glad to leave Mannion in safe hands, so it will be here, waiting for him, when he realises Australia has been a mistake and comes home.'

'This house is your passion, not his, Dana *mia*. He lives for surfing, and he is going to a place called Surfer's Paradise.'

He added sardonically, 'And I hope he does find it his personal Eden, as the PR world clearly has nothing more to offer him.'

'It's easy for you to sneer,' she hit back. 'The man who's always had everything. The apple of his father's eye.'

'We Belisandros have worked for what we have,' he said harshly. 'Fought to maintain our commercial eminence through succeeding economic crises. Never think it has been easy—not

with the futures of thousands of employees de-
pendent on the decisions we make each day. It
has been—essential.'

And living here is essential for me too, she
thought. I can't—I won't let it go. Not after all
these years of dreaming and planning.

But it was horribly apparent that she'd totally
misjudged the nature of Adam's 'serious talk'.

None of it made any sense, she thought. Neither Nic nor Adam had ever seemed sufficiently
enamoured of Sadie Latimer's family to want
any closer ties.

And while he was realising his error, she would
be the greatest live-in caretaker in the world.

All I have to do is convince him, she thought,
releasing her grip on the desk and flexing her
aching fingers.

'It's time I was gone,' she said, glancing at
her watch. 'And I mustn't detain you either,' she
added pointedly. 'I'm sure you have other places
to be—saving the economy.'

'No,' he said. 'I do not. Besides, I understood
you wished to talk to me and so far we have spoken only of Adam.'

'Mrs Harris has made a mistake,' she said. 'I asked for the master of the house.'

'Any misunderstanding is yours, *mia bella*,' he said. 'Because I have been the legal owner of this house and its land since noon today. So shall we open the champagne you so thoughtfully have brought and drink to Mannion's new beginning? Together?'

His dark face swam in front of her. She said in a choked voice, 'No, it's not true. He couldn't—he wouldn't...'

'Do you wish to see the papers? They are in that desk. Also Adam's receipt for the money. Well?'

She shook her head numbly and heard his sharp sigh.

He took her arm, shepherding her out of the room and across the hall to the drawing room where he placed her in the corner of a sofa and disappeared.

For a moment, Dana was completely still, then, with a soft moan, she buried her face in her hands, her body shaking with dry sobs.

Oh, God, she thought brokenly. The things

she'd said. The things she'd let him see. All in all, a pretty comprehensive exercise in self-betrayal.

But she must not make a bad situation worse. Somehow, she had to pull herself together and try to retrieve some of the ground she had lost.

When Zac returned with a tray of coffee, she'd combed her hair with her fingers and was sitting, quiet and composed, with her hands folded in her lap.

As he set down the tray, he said, 'Are you all right?'

'Yes.' Then: 'No! I don't see how he could do such a thing. Sell his inheritance.'

He shrugged, as he seated himself in a chair opposite. 'For money. Of course. Without winning the National Lottery, how else could he lay his hands on such a large sum with no real effort on his part?'

'But—Mrs Latimer—didn't she mind?'

'Serafina is a pragmatist. She made the gift as she believed her husband would have wished, but the rest was Adam's own business.'

She said, 'But why did he sell to you—of all people?'

'Ah,' he said softly. 'Then you have realised there is no love lost between us.'

She remembered the simmering resentment of the past weeks. 'Something like that.'

'Again, it was money. I offered the price he wanted, and it became a simple cash transaction without prolonged negotiations or expensive legal fees.' He added drily, 'He did not have to like me for it.'

'No.' Dana took a deep breath. 'But you—you really want Mannion?'

'It has its attractions. And I need a base apart from my London apartment.'

'So, it's just a matter of convenience.' She shook her head. 'Poor Mannion. All this was going on and I had no idea.' She paused. 'And you, of course, took the message I left. You didn't think of calling me—explaining the true situation?'

He said mockingly, 'Not even for a moment, *mia cara*. But I am sorry if I have deprived you of the celebration you had planned.'

'That doesn't matter.' Which was true. She felt nothing but relief that her surrender would not be required after all. Or that she might have to drink herself insensible first.

I didn't realise, she thought, how much I was actually dreading it.

Aloud, she said quickly, 'And I should go.'

'Not yet,' he said. 'It is unwise to drive after a shock.'

A shock, she thought bitterly. Was that really the way to describe the cataclysm that had just destroyed her dreams—her future, leaving her with nothing to hope for?

He poured the coffee, a rich, dark brew, and handed her a cup.

She lifted her chin. 'I prefer it with milk.'

'I suggest on this occasion you drink it black.' He leaned back, stretching out long legs in khaki chinos, his black polo shirt open at the neck. 'Because, Dana *mia*, you may need the extra caffeine when you hear what I have to say.'

CHAPTER NINE

SHE DIDN'T WANT COFFEE. The last thing she needed was an extra stimulant when she felt wired to snapping point already, but it seemed wiser to avoid a clash with her equally unwelcome host, so she drank some, finding she was oddly glad of its heat and strength.

'Goodness.' She tried to speak lightly to conceal her unease at his last remark. 'That sounds terribly serious.'

'Marriage,' he said, 'is a serious business.'

She replaced her cup carefully in its saucer. 'Yes, I—I suppose so. I didn't know you were contemplating such a thing.'

'I have thought of it for some time.'

'Your father must be pleased.'

'I think he will be,' he said. 'Eventually.'

She reached for her cup, needing to dispel the feeling of sick emptiness inside her, caused, she told herself, by the loss of Adam and, with him, Mannion.

Zac broke the silence. 'So,' he said, 'how would you save poor Mannion from being a mere convenience?'

'That's something you should discuss with your future wife.'

'Then be my wife,' he said lightly. 'And save Mannion from its fate.'

Her hand jerked, spilling coffee onto the coral dress. She said breathlessly, 'If that's a joke, I don't find it amusing.'

'I am perfectly serious,' he said. 'I am asking you to marry me, Dana *mia*.'

'In which case you must be mad.' She swallowed convulsively. 'And the answer is no.'

He sighed elaborately. 'And only moments ago you were declaring that no sacrifice was too great for the house you love.'

Oh, God, she thought. Why did I let my mouth run away with me?

She took a deep breath. 'Marriage is totally different. I am not for sale.'

Zac shrugged. 'Yet, to possess this house, you were ready to sell yourself to Adam.'

She stiffened. 'You have no right to suggest that. I'm involved in a relationship with him, as you know perfectly well.'

'So closely involved that you knew nothing of the Australian scheme.' It was a statement not a question.

She bit her lip. 'Perhaps he needed to be sure of the money before he told me.'

'Ah, yes,' Zac drawled. 'The money. He wishes, as always, to start at the top, with the expensive house and the lifestyle to match it.' He paused. 'So will he ask you to go with him to Australia and share his good fortune?' His dark gaze was quietly implacable. 'And, if so, will you agree— become his and leave everything else behind?'

There seemed little point in lying. Nor was there anywhere left for her to hide. She did not look at him, just shook her head, mutely, defeatedly.

'Then we understand each other. You want Mannion and I, *carissima mia*, want you.' He shrugged again, almost casually. 'In the end, it is very simple.'

'Simple,' Dana echoed incredulously. 'In what alternate universe is that?'

Her breathing had quickened and she saw that he was aware of it too, his eyes studying the rise and fall of her breasts. Her inner disturbance was turning to tumult. She touched the tip of her tongue to her dry lips, only to realise that was not lost on him either.

And knew that for her own safety, she should get out while she still could.

He said, 'It seems your desire for this house is not as strong as you implied.'

'There are ways of fulfilling it that don't involve marriage,' she said quickly. 'For instance, I'd be willing to work here as the housekeeper, as my aunt once did.'

'And put Signora Harris out of her job.' He tutted. 'That is hardly fair. And you know my terms. They will not change.' His smile was cynical. 'You were prepared to accept such an arrangement with Adam. At least you do not have to pretend to be in love with me.'

'Have you considered your father?' she asked almost desperately. 'He must expect you to marry someone more important than a housekeeper's illegitimate niece.'

'Perhaps, but he has always known that my wife would be my choice alone.'

'You seem to have an answer to everything,' Dana said bitterly.

'It is your answer that most concerns me. If I am so little to your taste, tell yourself you are really marrying Mannion, to have and to hold, to love and to cherish.' He paused. 'All you have to do is choose.'

The mockery in his voice was not lost on her.

He couldn't really mean to marry her—for the reasons she'd stated and more. Principally, because he was not the marrying kind.

It seemed far more likely that he was baiting her. Tempting her for his own amusement.

She knew, of course, what she wanted to say— needed to say. That she'd rather die than live with him. Allow him the intimacies he had a right to expect as her husband.

And he was waiting for her to say it. The slight derisive curl of his mouth as he watched her struggle told her so quite plainly.

And if—when—she damned him to hell and walked, she'd be once again leaving as a loser, this time with no way back.

My father's house, she thought, anguished. My birthright and my mother's vindication and ultimate happiness. I'll have lost it all. Everything...

'I am waiting,' he tormented softly.

She said, 'I need time to think...'

Zac shook his head. 'I require your answer now. Do we have a bargain—yes, or no?'

Mannion, she thought. Isn't that what really matters—that has to outweigh everything else?

She raised her head. Looked at him. She said huskily, 'Then I suppose—yes.' She hesitated. 'What happens now?'

She was waiting for him to laugh and tell her that he had indeed been joking. After which, she supposed, she would somehow have to leave with her head held high.

'I suggest a private civil ceremony with Nicola and Eddie as witnesses as soon as the necessary formalities are completed.'

Then it wasn't a laughing matter after all. He had it all worked out, she realised with disbelief.

And swallowed. 'Do we have to make an announcement? People will think it's so weird.'

'We do not have to concern ourselves with the opinions of others.'

'I'm sure you don't,' she said. 'Barricaded behind your security, your press office and your PR wall. I have to get on with my life. My job.'

'I fear Jarvis Stratton must become another sacrifice to Mannion. It would be best for you to hand in your notice—effective immediately, and vacate your flat.' His smile was ironic. 'Then join me behind the barricade.'

As her lips parted indignantly, he added, 'The matter is not open to debate.'

She drew a deep breath, 'You want us to—to live together—now.'

'No, *cara*, I will spare you that. From tomorrow, you will occupy the penthouse suite at the Capital Imperiale, where you met my father. I shall remain at my apartment—and count the hours,' he added softly. 'They say anticipation only increases the appetite. I shall enjoy discovering if that is true.'

Colour flared in Dana's face. She said unevenly, 'Please don't say things like that.'

She rose, feeling as if the ground was shifting under her feet. 'Now I suppose I must obey orders and go back to London to pack my things.'

She was halfway to the front door when she remembered something and turned, almost colliding with Zac who was close behind her.

'I beg your pardon.' She recovered herself with a gasp. 'I've left my case in the book room.'

Standing next to it, the champagne looked like a bad joke. Dana snatched at her case, only to realise with horror that she hadn't closed it properly after taking out the Cristal, and that everything it contained was now cascading to the carpet.

Including, of course, the sheer black nightgown, which had been a last-minute purchase that morning, born from a kind of desperation. A different sort of Dutch courage, she'd told herself.

Rooted to the spot, she watched Zac bend to pick it up, studying the shape of his hand through the transparent chiffon. And probably able to read his own fingerprints at the same time, she thought, biting her lip in an agony of embarrassment.

His voice like ice, he said, 'A celebration indeed.'

Rolling it into a ball, he tossed it to her. 'Please

do not think of wearing this for me.' He added, 'My tastes, you will find, are very different.'

He moved to the fireplace and rang the bell. 'Now you must excuse me. Signora Harris will see you out.'

Unable to look at him or speak, Dana bundled everything back into the case, and escaped.

Knowing, as she did so, that any freedom would only be temporary. And that she'd just committed herself to a giant leap into a terrifying unknown.

There were two messages on her machine at the flat, both of them from Nicola, sounding upset and wanting her to call back.

She's heard about Australia, thought Dana, and wants to talk about Adam. But I can't, because I don't know what to say. And, anyway, I have to try and make sense of today—if that's possible.

She stood for a moment in her living room, looking round her.

It wasn't large, a third of it occupied by the neat galley kitchen at one end, while the bedroom was even smaller, because some of its space had been used for an en-suite shower room. But, for a single person, it was fine and the rent was—just—affordable.

She'd painted the walls ivory and furnished with care, picking up a small sofa at auction, which she'd had re-covered in a rich William Morris fabric costing far more than the sofa itself. Her small Victorian kneehole desk, carefully cleaned and assiduously polished, had been a junk shop bargain.

Apart from a bookcase and a wall-mounted TV set, that was all. There were no pictures or ornaments to personalise it, as if she was reminding herself that it was not her home, and that she was just—passing through.

But she hadn't expected to be giving it up quite so soon, she thought, biting her lip as she carried her case through to the bedroom, and emptied it again, this time on purpose.

She found the balled-up nightgown and took it to the kitchen together with her coffee-stained dress which she'd exchanged for her bathrobe. Wrapping them both in carrier bags, she buried them deep in the garbage bin.

She washed her hands, then filled the kettle and set it to boil. She needed food too. Something to dispel the scared, hollow feeling inside her. There was a menu from a Chinese takeaway fastened to the fridge with a magnet, and she decided to order in once her packing was done. Not that there was much of it, apart from working gear. Pitifully little, in fact.

She supposed she'd have to buy a trousseau. Wasn't that what brides did? Except she wasn't a bride in the accepted sense—just part of a deal. But even that imposed certain practical obligations as well as those of an intimate nature that she didn't wish to contemplate.

Leaning against the worktop, she said slowly and clearly, 'I am going to be the wife of Zac Belisandro, one of the wealthiest men in Europe. I shall wear designer clothes, be hostess at his parties and appear at the kind of events I only read about in magazines at the hairdresser's.' Then waited in silence for her head to explode.

When it signally failed to do so, she made herself a mug of strong tea and went back to the bedroom, emptying the contents of the fitted wardrobe and drawers into the school suitcase she'd never bothered to replace.

No more choices, she thought. She'd take everything and probably keep none of it.

It was all done, and she was finishing her tea and glancing down the takeaway menu when her doorbell pealed abruptly.

Nicola, she thought resignedly. And she still couldn't think what to say to her. How to explain the most bizarre decision of her life.

She was still trying to come up with an opening gambit when she opened the door, and Adam walked in.

'So you are here,' was his irritated greeting. 'They said at Jarvis Stratton that you had a day off, but when I called round earlier, I got no answer. What's going on?'

Dana, about to close the door, turned instead to face him. 'Shouldn't that be my question?'

'Ah.' There was an awkward pause. 'So you've heard what I'm planning.'

'Planning,' she repeated. 'It's past that stage surely. I suppose you're here to say goodbye.'

'There's plenty of time for that.' He was recovering fast. Smiling. 'OK, maybe I should have said something.

'*Mea culpa.* But I've just made myself a small

fortune, so put on your glad rags and we'll go out. Paint the town crimson.'

'Thank you,' Dana said. 'But, no.' She hesitated. 'You wondered where I was today.'

He shrugged. 'What does it matter? You're here now.'

She said steadily, 'Actually, it does matter quite a lot. You see, Adam, I went down to Mannion this afternoon—to congratulate you on being its legal owner at last.'

'Oh, God,' he said and burst out laughing. 'And instead you found dear Cousin Zac, master of all he surveys. I thought you were looking a bit blue. Did he throw you out?'

No point in beating about the bush, she thought, drawing a deep breath. 'On the contrary, he asked me to stay—as his wife.'

The laughter stopped abruptly. He said, 'You are joking—right?'

'Wrong.' Her mouth felt dry. 'Zac proposed to me and I—I accepted him.' She lifted her chin. 'We're engaged.'

A silence. Then Adam said, cold and quietly, 'You sly, conniving little bitch. You money-grubbing greedy tart. It's that bloody house. You're fixated on it—would do anything to get it—just like your lying crackpot of a mother.'

Dana felt the blood draining from her face. She stared at him, shocked into silence, unable to produce a word in her own defence, if indeed there was anything to say.

'I knew I couldn't trust you,' the relentless voice went on. 'But I thought you'd learned your lesson seven years ago. Clearly, I was wrong.'

He paused. 'What I can't get my head round is how the hell you've got him to marry you. Why he hasn't just screwed you and walked away like he usually does.'

His smile was a sneer. 'The clever Mr Belisandro must be losing his grip. First he pays over the market price for an empty heap of stone in the middle of nowhere.

'Next, he'll have to explain to Papà Ottaviano and Cousin Serafina why he's polluting the Belisandro name by marrying the village whore's bastard.'

'Don't you *dare* talk about my mother like that.' Her voice shook.

'Don't give yourself airs,' he said. 'I've been a mug myself, letting you get away with the "hands off" treatment you've been giving me, while you've been opening your legs fast enough for Zac and his millions.'

He looked her over lasciviously, his eyes stripping away the towelling robe. 'So what's the going rate for demonstrating how you turn him on in bed? Give me something to remember you by when I'm far away? Zac wouldn't begrudge me a quickie. You're not the first woman we've shared.'

He took a step closer. 'So, what about it, sweetie? In the bedroom, or here on the floor?'

Dana said nothing, just lifted her hand and slapped him so hard across the face that the blow jarred her arm up to the shoulder.

For a moment, he was silent, glaring at her, then he said thickly, 'You're going to regret that.'

'No,' Zac said from the doorway. 'But you will unless you leave now.'

Dana whirled, staring at him, wanting suddenly to run to him. To bury her face against his chest and feel him holding her. Making her safe.

Except that was madness. Zac's arms were no security zone. She would simply be leaping out of the frying pan into a blazing fire.

Besides, the ugly brutality of Adam's words and all they implied was keeping her motionless and nauseated. Words that Zac must have heard during his noiseless approach.

She could feel the violence in the room, hot and heavy, as Adam's mouth stretched in another sneer. 'You really think you can make me?'

'No,' Zac said softly. 'I don't think. I know. So walk, unless you want to be thrown down the stairs.'

For a moment, Adam's gaze was murderous, then, with a shrug, he walked past Zac and was gone, leaving them with the sound of his feet descending the stairs in the conventional manner.

Zac slammed the door and looked at Dana, his eyes cold as he surveyed the bathrobe. 'Why was he here?'

'I thought he was Nicola and he just—walked in. He wanted to take me out so I—I told him about—us and he freaked.' She swallowed. 'That's all it was. Truly.'

Zac sighed, pushing his hair back from his face with a restless hand. 'I was parking my car when I saw him drive up. I thought—*Dio*—what did I not think?' He shook his head. 'Then I heard him—that filth he was saying.' He smiled thinly. 'And I saw your reaction, *mia cara*.'

'It's as if I never knew him.' Dana looked at the floor. 'He became some—ghastly stranger.' Her voice cracked. 'It was—horrible.'

'It is over,' he said. 'And nothing happened. However, I shall not wait for tomorrow, but take you to the hotel tonight.'

She knew she should come up with a token protest at the very least. Pride demanded it.

Except she was lucky to have any pride left. And if she remained at the flat, there was no guarantee that Adam would not return. Even the possibility made her feel sick.

She swallowed. 'If you hadn't arrived when you did…' She paused. 'Why is that, anyway? I thought you were staying at Mannion.'

'I intended to do so,' Zac returned levelly. 'But our parting was not as I would have wished.'

She looked away. 'Have you changed your mind about the—the bargain?'

'No.' His brows lifted. 'Our agreement still stands. Why should you doubt it?'

'I suppose because nothing about today seems

quite real.' She hesitated. 'Adam said he made you pay too much for Mannion.'

He shrugged. 'I paid what it was worth to me.'

'And could you really have thrown him downstairs?'

'Why, yes, *mia bella.* Quite easily and enjoyed doing so.' He smiled faintly. 'Or did you think you had a monopoly on violent gestures?'

She shuddered. 'I've never hit anybody in my life before.'

'No,' he said quietly. 'But you would often have liked to, I think.'

Flushing, she met the amused challenge in his gaze. 'Perhaps.'

For a long moment, her eyes were locked with his, then Zac looked away, glancing round him. 'Your apartment is charming.' He paused. 'I presume the furniture belongs to you? Do you wish to have it at Mannion?'

'I hadn't thought that far ahead,' she confessed. 'But maybe the desk and the sofa, if there's space for them. And my books. Everything else can go to a charity shop.'

'I will make the necessary arrangements tomorrow.'

'Thank you.' She hesitated. 'As a matter of interest, how did you know where I lived?'

'I made it my business to know,' he said laconically. 'Now get dressed, finish your packing and we will go.'

'What about my car?'

'I will have that collected tomorrow and brought to the hotel.'

Like waving a magic wand, Dana thought rebelliously as she went into the bedroom to change.

It was a silent journey to the hotel. Dana stood tensely beside Zac in the lift as it whisked them swiftly and silently to the penthouse.

She hadn't really appreciated its magnificence on her first visit, she thought as she looked around her. She'd been too thrown by finding herself confronting Signor Ottaviano.

'I hope you will be comfortable here,' Zac said courteously. 'Whatever you require, you have only to pick up the phone and ask.'

'An hour ago I was starving,' she said. 'Now I seem to have lost my appetite.'

'You have had a disturbing day,' he said. 'I will order some hot chocolate for you, and then I suggest an early night.' He saw her stiffen and smiled sardonically. 'But not with me, *carissima*. I hope that reassures you.'

'Yes,' she said. 'I mean—no. I don't need reassurance.' She paused. 'What did you mean earlier— about our parting?'

'We will discuss it another time.' His tone was dismissive. 'Now, I will let you rest. *A domani*, Dana *mia*. Until tomorrow.'

She watched him walk away across the room, her mind teeming. Knowing there was something she needed to say, but unable to find the words.

It was only when the door had closed behind him that she heard herself whispering, almost desperately, 'Don't leave me. Don't go.'

And felt herself reel in shocked disbelief at her own stupidity.

CHAPTER TEN

'ARE YOU ABSOLUTELY sure about this?' said Nicola, her face anxious. 'I'm not defending Adam—I think he's behaved abominably and not for the first time—but Zac is seriously not the kind of man you marry on the rebound. And if you're having any second thoughts, maybe now's the time to say so.'

Second thoughts, third thoughts and every other kind of thought there is, Dana returned silently. But they've changed nothing.

Aloud, she said, 'It isn't a bit like that, I promise.'

Although, she thought ruefully, she was damned if she knew what it was like.

She added, 'And Adam is perfectly entitled to make a new life in Australia.'

Nicola snorted wrathfully. 'If that was all! But you haven't heard what he's been saying—bad-mouthing Zac to anyone who'll listen. I'd almost forgotten how vindictive he can be when he lets that Mr Charm image slip.' She paused. 'Yet you saw how he was with Aunt Mimi.'

'Yes.' And with me, Dana thought, biting her lip.

'He felt she'd made him look a fool, and he could never stand that,' Nicola went on. 'And he was furious with me for inviting you for that weekend. Said he thought he'd made sure you were the last person he'd ever see again.'

She pulled a face. 'And he went ballistic when he discovered Eddie and I were still being married from Mannion. I didn't dare say that Zac had asked us to be the witnesses at your wedding.'

'I expect you're wise,' Dana said carefully. 'Now calm down and have some more tea. And another cream cake.'

Nicola surveyed the loaded trolley which had been ceremoniously wheeled into the suite some fifteen minutes before and groaned. 'Don't tempt me.' She gave Dana a quizzical look. 'How does it feel to be living in the lap of luxury?'

Dana forced a smile. 'I suppose—luxurious. Would you like the guided tour?'

'Tea in the sitting room is one thing,' said

Nicola, glancing towards the bedroom. 'But invading Zac's privacy is quite another. I'll pass.'

'My privacy actually,' said Dana. 'Zac is living at his flat.'

'Good God,' Nicola said blankly. 'And I thought the whole reason for this high-speed, low-key wedding was your total inability to keep your hands off each other.

'After all the world would expect the Belisandro heir to be married by some cardinal in a packed cathedral.'

'Then the world would be wrong,' Dana said brightly. 'Because it will be just the four of us at the registry office, making it a very small day. Zac's father doesn't approve of civil marriages and Mrs Latimer has just had an operation, so Aunt Joss doesn't feel she can leave her.'

'And your mother?' Nicola asked gently.

'I wrote, inviting her, but she hasn't replied.' Dana bent her head. 'When Aunt Joss finally gave me her address in Spain, she warned me I'd be wasting my time.' She sighed. 'But at least I know where she is—working in a place called Roberto's Bar in Altamejo. It doesn't sound too promising.'

Nicola grimaced sympathetically. 'Well, my mother won't be gracing my wedding either. But she and lover-boy have sent me the most incredible emerald bracelet as a wedding present. One look and Eddie took it straight to the bank.'

She paused. 'So what are you planning to wear at this very quiet wedding?'

'Nothing,' said Dana without thinking and Nicola gurgled with laughter.

'Well, I'd have to blindfold Eddie, and the registrar, but Zac would probably be delighted.'

Dana groaned. 'You can joke,' she said. 'But I've been searching through every department store in London, and I can't find anything remotely suitable.'

'Then we'll go together. I know loads of places,' Nicola said confidently. 'You'd better make a list. I suppose you're going somewhere exotic on honeymoon so you'll need beachwear and pretty floaty things for the evenings.'

'Actually, no,' Dana said reluctantly. 'We aren't having a honeymoon—or not immediately. Zac will be travelling to Europe almost at once, dealing with the problems thrown up at the conference. And as it will be wall to wall meetings, starting at breakfast and going on until late into the night, I'll be staying at Mannion.'

She smiled. 'Making sure all the refurbishment is done in time for your wedding.'

'To blazes with that,' Nicola said vigorously. 'You should be with Zac on this European tour. He must surely intend to go to bed at some point between meetings, and sex, quite apart from anything else, is a great stress buster.'

Dana forced a smile. 'I get the impression he thrives on stress. Anyway, he's quite adamant. He goes. I stay.'

And she was thankful for it, she told herself when Nicola had departed and she was alone again, remembering Zac's slanting smile as he gave her the news, adding softly, 'So, for a while, you will be spared my constant company, *mia bella*.'

Although she would still have to undergo the ordeal of their wedding night and all those other nights before he left. There was no escape from that.

As Zac had reminded her. 'The interior design of the house, Dana *mia*, is your domain.' Adding softly, 'As you will be mine.'

Because their marriage was only a trade. Her body for his house.

That's what he was telling her again. What his touch had said long before the startling moment when he'd proposed to her and been accepted.

So why, in that case, was she still sleeping alone in a bed as wide as the ocean?

Not that she wanted anything else, she added hastily. But this delaying of the inevitable was making her nervous.

I don't understand it, she thought. I don't understand *him*.

Was it forbearance, sparked by some innate awareness of her inexperience, or was he playing a cat and mouse game with her senses? Keeping her deliberately on a knife-edge of uncertainty?

Whichever—it ultimately made no difference. Because she would never be his in the way that Mannion would be hers. Never belong to him, because she already belonged to Mannion.

And nothing, she told herself defiantly, would ever change that.

It was a very conventional ring. Just a plain circlet created from a modest lump of gold, not wide enough to reach her knuckle, or studded with precious stones.

Something she'd not expected, like the way Zac had touched the gold to his lips before slipping it on to her finger.

It felt alien on her hand, its gleam always catching her eye, she thought, nervously smoothing the cream silk of her wedding dress over her knees.

Nicola had been as good as her word, taking her on a whirlwind tour of more boutiques and small designer shops than Dana had known existed, and firmly refusing to listen to her 'no honeymoon' excuses.

'If he's going to be away, all the more reason to welcome him back in something glamorous,' she'd ordained sternly.

So Dana had capitulated, albeit reluctantly. But she had to admit, after years of strict budgeting, it was fun to splurge on the kind of clothes she'd never expected to afford, let alone wear.

Her wedding dress had been her first purchase. She'd noticed it at once, half hidden in an array of glittering evening wear, catching her breath as she lifted it from the rail.

It was a simple slip of a dress, figure-skimming

but beautifully cut, with a low square bodice and cap sleeves, and the moment she'd tried it on, she knew it was the one.

She'd stared at herself in the dressing room mirror, seeing a girl with flushed cheeks and eyes alight with excitement. And for an instant had allowed herself to wonder how Zac would see her. What he would think.

Well, she now had the answer to that, which was—very little. His face as she entered the wedding room had been expressionless. She'd thanked him haltingly for the exquisite bouquet of cream roses he'd sent her and he'd simply replied, *'Di niente,'* then turned to the registrar, who was waiting to begin.

After they'd exchanged vows, he'd bent and brushed her mouth with his, so lightly and formally that it was hardly a kiss at all.

Over the lunch at the Ritz with Nic and Eddie which followed, he'd been a faultlessly charming host. But now they were alone, they'd shared a well nigh silent journey.

Perhaps it had occurred to him that this hasty marriage might not be the best idea he'd ever had, Dana thought, her throat tightening in sudden, sharp desolation. And if so, what would she do? Or rather, she amended hastily, what would happen to Mannion?

But if he'd changed his mind about their bargain, he'd had plenty of time to say so prior to the wedding. Especially as they'd already had what almost amounted to their first quarrel when Dana had learned he intended them to occupy the great master bedroom.

'You decided this without asking me?' she'd flung at him. 'When there are so many other rooms? Why that one?'

'Because it is the master bedroom,' he'd returned coldly. 'And, like it or not, Dana *mia*, I mean to be the master.'

He'd studied her flushed, mutinous face. 'Or do you anticipate finding Adam's shadow falling across our bed? It will not, I promise you.'

Her colour had deepened not with guilt but annoyance. Because, she realised bitterly, a simple denial that Adam, now safely in Australia, had ever entered her mind would sound as lame as the actual truth—that she'd never liked the room with its massive four-poster bed and deep crimson wallpaper, even when it was occupied by Serafina. That she'd always found it gloomy and oppressive.

But he hadn't consulted her. So much for the house being her domain, she thought biting her lip. Whatever decisions she might make, Zac would always have the power to overrule her.

My master too, she'd thought angrily. In every way.

And when she spoke, her tone was curt, disguising the fact that her throat had closed in panic. 'Think what you like.'

She knew that he too was angry, and their parting that evening had been cool.

And there'd been no sign since that he'd rethought his decision.

For the first time, her usual sense of excitement when she saw Mannion from the top of the hill was replaced by apprehension.

When they reached the drive, she could see a team of men working in the garden, which was almost back to its old pristine condition. Mr Godstow, now retired, would have been proud, she thought.

Zac parked the car at the main entrance and

came round to open the passenger door, handing Dana her bouquet from the back seat.

The door was standing open and Dana could see Mrs Harris waiting in the hall to greet them. But she'd hardly taken a step when Zac swept her up into his arms and carried her over the threshold into the house.

On the point of struggling, Dana remembered just in time that they had an audience.

She was aware too of Zac whispering something in her ear before he set her on her feet but she was too unnerved by finding herself held so closely to make out what he'd said.

Mrs Harris stepped forward. 'It's very good to see you, sir, and you, madam,' she said. 'All the work you requested has been done, and I hope you'll find it satisfactory. May I say, also, that I wish you and Mrs Belisandro every happiness.'

She paused, looking awkward. 'And there's a Mr Fleming waiting in the book room, sir. I believe he's expected.'

'I will see him now,' Zac said. 'While you show my wife to our room.' He took Dana's nerveless hand and kissed it lightly. 'A matter of business,

but I shall not keep you waiting long, *mia cara*,'
he added softly.

She stammered something and turned almost
precipitately to follow the housekeeper up the
stairs, her mind whirling.

Surely, she thought, he didn't mean that as it
sounded.

She'd thought she'd be allowed a breathing
space.

Time to adjust to this new and difficult situation.

But she could hardly protest. This, after all, was
what she'd signed up to. And Zac was a business-
man. Whether it was day or night, he would expect his money's worth.

They had reached their destination, she realised, and Mrs Harris was throwing open the
door with something of a flourish, and standing
back to allow Dana to precede her into the room.

'I do hope you'll be pleased, madam.'

A better word would be 'astounded,' Dana
thought as she looked around her. Because she
barely recognised her new surroundings.

The great canopied bed had gone, along with
the rest of the enormous dark furniture, to be

replaced by a wide, low divan, with an elegant headboard in the same pale honey-coloured wood as the pretty antique dressing table and the night tables flanking the bed.

The walls were now ivory, as were the curtains at the long windows, which were embellished with a delicate tracery of leaves and flowers in gold, a design matched by the bedcover.

'So nice that this room is being used again,' said Mrs Harris. 'Mr Adam, of course, preferred to sleep in his old room, but, even so, I was sorry when he decided to get rid of the bed, although it wasn't my place to say so. But the room's certainly more cheerful without it.'

She walked across to a door. 'Your bathroom and dressing room are through here, madam. Mr Belisandro's dressing room and shower are reached by that door opposite.

'It's been a real rush getting everything ready,' she went on. 'But I think it's been worth it.'

'Yes,' Dana said rather faintly. 'It's—beautiful. Absolutely amazing.'

Mrs Harris beamed at her. 'Mr Belisandro will be glad to hear that, madam. He insisted that everything be exactly right for you.'

'He's—very considerate,' Dana agreed quietly.

She became aware that she was still clutching her roses, and Mrs Harris noticed it too.

'May I put those in water for you, madam, while you have a proper look round?'

'Why, yes. Thank you.' Dana surrendered her bouquet to the housekeeper, who bustled away with it.

Investigation showed that her part of the suite had been created from the adjoining large bedroom.

She could not fault the dressing room, lined with fitted wardrobes on one side and drawers and smaller cupboards on the other, already filled with the trousseau that had been sent down two days earlier. While the bathroom beyond it was a dream, with its deep tub and roomy shower, all enclosed in tiles gleaming like mother-of-pearl, and giving the impression that she would be bathing in an enormous shell.

As she returned to the bedroom, she glanced across at the other door, but decided against investigating what arrangements Zac had made for himself, telling herself just to be glad that they were separate.

She wandered over to the dressing table and studied herself in its mirror. She was sure most brides didn't look so wide-eyed and nervous or have lines of strain etched beside their mouths.

It occurred to her that until now she'd been cocooned in an aura of unreality, telling herself that she would never be called on to ratify her unholy bargain.

Yet here she was. And with no one to blame but herself for her predicament.

She wondered, with a sudden shiver, how she'd be feeling if her original plan had worked. If it was Adam with the right to share that bed and impose his demands on her.

Except it would never have happened, she thought slowly. Because somewhere along the way the real Adam would have surfaced and I'd have run, even though it meant losing Mannion.

And that being the case, why didn't I tell Zac I'd changed my mind and get out while I still could?

Only to realise, as if some veil in her mind had been suddenly torn aside, the truth she'd been hiding from for the past seven years.

And exactly why she was standing here now, waiting for her husband to join her.

CHAPTER ELEVEN

DANA TURNED AWAY from the mirror, shivering. Rejecting the image of this stranger who had shocked her into more emotional turmoil than she'd ever dreamed possible.

I don't want to know her, she thought desperately as she began to tremble. I don't understand where she's come from. I only know that I can't afford to live in her head—or her heart.

Because to think how she thinks—to feel what she might feel—would be utter madness. Besides, it's not true—any of it. It can't be...

It was better—safer to believe what she was experiencing was simply a recurrence of an old dangerous obsession that she'd believed—prayed—was dealt with and gone.

It had started in the first awful weeks of her banishment from Mannion, as she lay crying herself to sleep each night, hating the injustice of it all. Hating Zac for making a fool of her, then lying about it. Hating him for the dreams she was ashamed to remember in the morning.

They talked about people adding insult to injury, but in her case the opposite was true. Zac's cynical attempt at seduction, pretending to be Adam, had been the insult.

But accusing her of being some kind of teenage nymphomaniac and having her dismissed from Mannion had been the ultimate injury, for which she would never forgive him.

As the days passed, she'd become unhappily accustomed to her small, hot room at the top of the house, the London traffic noise which never seemed to stop, and even the spoiled whiny children. Most of the time she was able to shut it all out of her mind.

But not Zac Belisandro. He was always there in her head. She found herself almost feverishly scanning the papers for news about Belisandro International and the man they'd christened the Playboy Tycoon, waiting, hoping to read that his life had crashed and burned too.

Instead, he'd seemed to go from strength to strength, in the personal as well as the business sense. The glossy magazines were full of the girls he was dating—usually for weeks, but sometimes, recalling a beautiful French actress and a blonde American model, for months.

It was then that the dreams started again, but this time with herself an unwilling bystander, unable to move, forced to watch him with a series of strangers in his arms.

Common sense told her to give up what almost amounted to an addiction. To stop looking for his name in the news columns and on the internet.

Instead, she'd told herself defensively that she needed to keep tabs on him—to know where he was living, and the places he frequented so she could avoid them. So she could make sure she never bumped into him, even by chance.

His move to the Melbourne office had been like the unlocking of a cage.

I'm free at last, she'd told herself, almost exultant with relief. And one of the chief barriers to Mannion has been removed too. My life is going to change.

And so it had—but in a way she'd never imagined possible.

I want you...

Three little words, blunt and unequivocal, without any gloss of tenderness.

Was that how Zac would be with her—greedy and uncaring—intent solely on his own pleasure?

She told herself that she wished she could think so.

That she longed to believe that the beguilement of his mouth, the whisper of his fingers on her skin meant nothing more than a fixed determination to have his way with her. And that any kind of response from her was not a requirement of the transaction.

It was, she thought, her only hope of a reprieve from what, she now realised with stunning force, was the very real threat of self-betrayal.

I can't let that happen, she whispered silently. Even when I was a young girl, I recognised the power he had, and it scared me. So, I can't allow him to control me now. I have to resist. Fight him. And fight myself.

Forget there was a wedding today and treat it as a mere business transaction. And hope that Zac soon becomes bored and starts looking for other interests.

Because to wish for anything else would be madness.

She turned to get out of this room with all its connotations and halted, gasping when she saw that Zac was standing in the doorway to his dressing room, hands on hips, his coat and tie discarded, his shirt unbuttoned almost to the waist, with its sleeves turned back over his forearms.

His appearance might be casual but, to Dana, it made him no less formidable.

She said, her voice breathless, 'I thought you'd be still engaged with your visitor. You—you startled me.'

'So I saw,' Zac returned drily. 'And my visitor came only to make a delivery.' He strolled forward. 'Perhaps, in future, I should signal my arrival by whistling loudly, or shouting *Hi!* What do you think?'

She shrugged defensively. 'That it's probably best to leave things as they are. After all, they say you can become accustomed to anything in time.'

'I wonder if marriage is included in that generalisation,' he said musingly, and paused. 'So, as a beginning, can you become used to the changes in this room, *mia cara*?'

'I would prefer to have been consulted,' she said, casting a coolly appraising look around her. 'You did say the house was my domain.'

Ungrateful, she thought, hating herself. Ungrateful and ungracious.

His brows lifted. 'Then I apologise. I hoped it would be a pleasant surprise for you. And that it might make the room, you understand, more acceptable.'

Yes, she understood, and knew that if this was a real marriage and she was here for the right reasons, she'd have been in his arms by now, whispering *'Grazie'* between kisses.

As it was, she needed more than ever to stick to the path she'd chosen.

'On the subject of surprises,' she went on. 'Was it really necessary to carry me into the house in front of Mrs Harris? I could have walked.'

'Blame my Roman ancestry, *mia bella*,' Zac drawled. 'If a bride stumbled on the threshold of her new home in ancient times, it was considered a great misfortune, so it was deemed better to carry her.'

'And, of course, our situation is so perfect,' Dana said tautly. 'Besides which, I have always regarded Mannion as my own home, as I'm sure you know.'

His mouth tightened, but when he spoke, his tone was pleasant. 'Then put the incident down as an irresistible impulse, *carissima*.'

'You said something too. What was it?'

'Another old custom. I said, *"Ubi tu Gaia, ego Gaius."* It means "Wherever you are mistress, I am master."'

'Not everywhere,' Dana said. 'Just here in this house. But thank you for the history lesson.'

'If I did not know better,' Zac remarked softly, 'I would think you were trying to pick a quarrel with me, Dana *mia*.' He paused. 'I am permitted to presume that you are mine, I hope, or will that prove another bone of contention?'

She bit her lip, and he sighed. 'Shall we declare a truce for a while? I have been sent to tell you there is tea on the terrace.' He paused. 'Unless you would prefer to remain here and wait for dinner, which I have ordered for eight o clock.'

But would she be waiting alone?

'Tea,' she said, 'would be lovely.'

It was deliciously warm on the terrace and Zac was clearly relaxed, leaning back against the cushions, his dark gaze offering frank appreciation of the first smooth roundness of her breasts revealed by her dress. She might resent his scrutiny, but it was trivial compared with the realisation that, in a few short hours, Zac would have the right to see her wearing nothing at all.

'When I return from my tour,' he said, 'my father wishes us to join him at our house on Lake Como. I believe he wishes us to have our marriage blessed in the family chapel.'

'Under the circumstances, that seems almost blasphemous.' Dana lifted her chin. 'And anyway, I can't be away. I have far too much to do here.'

He sat up. 'You cannot spare my father a few days to welcome you as a daughter?'

'I didn't realise our deal contracted me to play happy families,' she returned coolly.

'Then you know it now.' His tone did not encourage further argument. 'In return, I am happy to accompany you to Spain to visit your mother.'

She looked down at her hands, tightly clasped

in her lap. She said quietly, 'Thank you, but that won't be necessary.'

He said nothing, but she had a sense of harsh anger, rigidly controlled, and began to feel angry herself. Hadn't Linda suffered enough without having to endure Serafina's cousin of all people invading her Spanish sanctuary?

Anger was good, she told herself. So was resentment. Feeding them would prevent foolish thoughts. Crazy longings...

She said tautly, 'And Mrs Latimer? I can't imagine she'll be welcoming me to Italy in any guise. Or that she'll forgive either of us for the fact that I'm now occupying her home.'

'To begin with,' he said, 'this house ceased to be a home for her after the deaths of her husband and her only son. It became an empty shell that she was glad to leave, nor did she care who would live here after her.'

A heap of stone in the middle of nowhere...

Adam had said that, she thought. But it wasn't true. It would never be true. She would see to that.

'And when you meet again,' Zac added, 'she

will expect you to call her Serafina as I do. *Capito?*'

'Yes,' she said. 'I understand.'

'And resent it, I think.' His voice was suddenly rueful. 'So let me share with you some news that will please you better. Your car has arrived. My driver brought it down a short while ago.' He took the key from his pocket and placed it on the table between them. 'No doubt you are glad to have it again.'

'Yes,' she said slowly, picking up the key and weighing it in her hand. 'Yes, I am.'

'You see it as a means of escape, perhaps?' He shook his head. 'It will not happen.'

'You'd stop me?'

'No. Simply trust you, *mia bella*, to honour our agreement to the full.'

'"Honour",' she repeated bitterly. 'That's a strange word to use in this context.'

'You should have thought of that,' he said. 'Before you allowed me to place my wedding ring on your hand this morning.'

He allowed her to absorb that then sighed abruptly.

'Perhaps, Dana *mia*, it would do us both good

to cool off a little.' He got to his feet and held out his hand to her. 'I am going for a swim. Will you come with me?'

Dana stiffened as she was assailed by an inconvenient memory—an image of Zac leaving the water, bronzed and naked. It seemed highly unlikely that he planned to wear anything this time either.

'No, thank you,' she said tersely. 'I'm quite comfortable as I am.'

'If a little flushed,' he said, a faint smile playing around his mouth.

'And I'm not a good swimmer,' she went on hurriedly.

Zac shrugged. '*Non importa.* I am not likely to let you drown.'

'Even so,' she said. 'The answer is still no.'

'*Sì, carissima,*' he said softly. 'But to how many questions?'

And he turned away, walking down the steps and heading off in the direction of the Orangery, leaving her staring after him.

Left alone, Dana made herself drink her tea and eat a sandwich and a slice of cake. An attempt at normality in what, by anyone's standards, was an abnormal situation.

Her best plan, she decided, would be to concentrate on something completely different. Keep busy by finding somewhere she could establish as a workplace and make a start on her real purpose for being here.

And she would start by changing into everyday gear, she thought, rising to her feet.

A short while later, wearing denim Capri pants and a white shirt knotted at the midriff, she came back on to the terrace, where Mrs Harris was clearing the tea things.

As she turned to go into the house, Dana halted her. 'Mrs Harris, have a desk and sofa been delivered for me by any chance?'

'They are due to arrive tomorrow, madam. Mr Belisandro has ordered the morning room to be cleared to make room for them.'

Dana smiled pleasantly, 'Well, I may have ideas of my own about that,' she said, heading for the terrace steps.

For a long time, she'd regarded the summer house as a strictly no-go area but that was ending right now, she told herself as she walked across the lawn.

After all, whatever memories it held would soon be superseded by others far more potent, leaving her free to treat it as no more than an extension to the house.

Her private sanctuary, in fact, with her own furniture.

It would need work, of course. Electricity was an absolute essential.

No more being left in the dark, she told herself grimly.

The path up to it seemed much narrower, and the trees and shrubs which flanked it had been allowed to grow unchecked, so much so that they concealed any view of the building.

Then as she rounded the final corner, she saw why. Because where the summer house had stood, there was now just empty space, the ground churned up as if it had been ploughed with not even a wooden plank remaining.

Dana stared at the desolation, feeling as if all the wind had been knocked out of her.

Why? she thought. In God's name—why?

She turned and plunged back down the slope.

When she reached the lawn again, one of the gardeners was emerging from the shrubbery, pushing a wheelbarrow and she accosted him.

'Can you tell me what happened to the summer house?'

'Pulled down and carted away, miss. Boss's orders.' He paused. 'Old Mr Godstow tried to talk him out of it, seemingly, but he wouldn't listen. Just said he'd always hated the bloody place—except he didn't say bloody.'

'I see,' Dana said numbly, but it wasn't true and her immediate instinct was to find Zac, wet or dry, and demand to know the reason for this cruel act of vandalism.

But, halfway to the swimming pool, she halted, realising she couldn't ask any such thing. Couldn't let him know that the summer house mattered, or why she was left hurt and bewildered at its destruction.

Far better not to mention it, she decided unhappily. And if he did, pretend total indifference.

After all, what was one more pretence among so many?

I need to forget the past, she told herself as she turned towards the house, and concentrate on the future. On bringing Mannion back to life. Because that's why I'm here and it's all that can be allowed to matter.

Accompanied by Mrs Harris and armed with a notebook and pen, Dana began upstairs, deciding which of the bedrooms needed to be completely redecorated and which only needed new curtains and bedding.

'I'm afraid this wedding is going to involve you in a lot of work, Mrs Harris,' she said apologetically.

'On the contrary, madam, I'm looking forward to it. Such a lovely girl, Miss Nicola.' The other woman beamed. 'And Mr Belisandro has arranged for me to have help with the cleaning— Mrs Cawston from the village will be coming every weekday from now on and she has a niece who can help out in emergencies.'

'That is good news,' Dana agreed. 'Now I think I'd better let you go as you'll be wanting to get on with dinner.'

'That's all done,' Mrs Harris assured her. She went a little pink. 'And Mr Belisandro told me you will serve yourselves and has given me the evening off.'

'Oh,' said Dana, flushing in turn. 'Oh, of course.'

As she went downstairs, she decided it might be time to make friends with the morning room, as it now seemed likely she'd be spending much of her time there.

But as she passed the book room, Zac was just emerging. He said, 'I was coming to find you. We need to talk a little about money.'

On the desk, Dana saw an array of platinum credit cards, a very large chequebook and a green folder containing a sheaf of papers, neatly clipped together.

She said, 'I do already have a credit card and a chequebook.'

'*Naturalamente.* But in order to run Mannion, you will also need these. As well as the usual household expenses, there are wages to pay, and of course the cost of your redecoration programme.' He indicated the file. 'All the details are here, and you will need to give the bank a specimen of your signature—in your married name.'

She nodded. 'I presume your instructions include an upper limit?'

Zac shrugged. '*Al contrario,* spend whatever

you wish.' He added softly, 'My side of our bargain, *carissima*.'

Our bargain, Dana thought. That ugly, evil thing she'd seized on so blindly—to satisfy the desire to possess which had dominated her life since childhood.

Money-grubbing greedy tart. Adam's vicious words—coming back to flay the skin from her body, because she could no longer deny their truth. Or the shame of them.

And telling herself that, as Jack Latimer's daughter, Mannion should have been hers anyway no longer worked. Because the end did not—could not—justify the means she had chosen.

She said in a voice she hardly recognised, 'You're—very generous.'

'Why not?' he said, and the cynical note in his voice made her flinch. 'When I expect to be so exquisitely rewarded.'

He paused. 'You have changed out of your beautiful dress. Why?'

'I had things to do and thought working gear would be more appropriate. Anyway, I didn't know you'd noticed my dress,' she added without thinking.

His brows lifted. 'You imagine I am blind?'

'No. It—it was a stupid thing to say. And I wasn't fishing for a compliment either.'

His smile was swift and ironic. 'Or, at least, not from me. I need no reminder of that.'

He paused. 'May I suggest we eat quite soon? You touched little of your lunch and almost nothing since then.'

So he hadn't just noticed her dress, thought Dana, her throat tightening. She would have to make a show of enjoying dinner, or he would think she was on hunger strike.

She said with unaccustomed meekness, 'Yes, a meal would be good.'

And, to her surprise, it was.

They dined on chilled avocado soup, followed by salmon mayonnaise and rounded off by a delicate lemon mousse with fresh raspberries. All of it accompanied by a crisp, fragrant white wine which was new to her.

But which might prove her salvation, she thought, recklessly downing her first glass.

'Have a care, *mia cara*,' Zac cautioned softly as she embarked on the second. 'This is an exquisite vintage, not an anaesthetic.'

She bit her lip. 'I don't know what you mean.'

'I am relieved to hear it.' He paused. 'I heard today there is another name to add to the guest list for the wedding. My cousin Serafina has decided to attend. As you know, she has a great fondness for Nicola.'

But not for me, thought Dana, replacing her glass carefully on the table. 'Is she well enough for the journey?'

'She is now walking with a stick and expects to be fully recovered by the wedding. Your aunt will, of course, be accompanying her,' he added. 'And their rooms should be adjacent, if that is possible.'

Dana looked down at the table. She said quietly, 'I'll see to it.'

It occurred to her that it could be an awkward reunion on both fronts, and she sighed inwardly.

'Would you like coffee?' Zac asked when the meal was over.

'No, thank you,' she said, just managing to stop herself saying, 'It keeps me awake.'

He watched her meditatively. When he spoke, his voice was gentle. 'Will you believe me if I tell you there is nothing to fear?'

'No,' she said. 'How can I?'

Because what really frightens me is what might happen when you touch me. When you discover that seven years ago you taught me to want you in return. And that, heaven help me, I haven't forgotten…

'But it makes no difference,' she went on, her voice husky, hurried. 'We made a bargain, and I'll keep my side of it. You—you can do what you want and I won't stop you.'

'*Carissima.*' His voice was oddly gentle. Even coaxing. 'I have had more enticing offers.'

'And will again, I'm sure,' she said stonily, as pain, swift and surprising, lanced through her. 'But not from me. Never from me. Whatever you said earlier, you—you can't really expect that.'

'I anticipated I would need patience,' he said. 'It seems I was right.'

He pushed back his chair. 'I, however, will have coffee and then complete some work for my trip. I will join you in three-quarters of an hour. Is that acceptable?'

She seemed suddenly unable to frame the word 'Yes' so she merely nodded as she rose from the table.

Leaving the room, she seemed to feel his gaze following her—touching her like a hand on her shoulder as she climbed the stairs to the room and the bed she was about to share with him.

CHAPTER TWELVE

THE BED HAD been turned down, she saw, and one of her new nightgowns, a demure white lawn affair, had been arranged on the coverlet.

She ran herself a warm bath, testing the array of expensive toiletries awaiting her, and eventually scenting the water with rose geranium.

When she was dry, she slipped the nightgown over her head and went back to the bedroom, sitting at the dressing table to brush her hair.

As she put the brush down, she heard his dressing room door open and rose, turning to face him, her hands clenched at her sides, her body, in its opaque veiling unyielding as a statue and as still.

Zac halted and, for a long moment, they stared at each other across the room.

Then, with a harsh sigh, he walked across to the bed, discarding the white towelling robe which proved to be his only garment, offering her an unwanted reminder of how magnificent he looked naked, and slid under the covers.

'If you wish to stand there all night, like some virgin martyr at the stake, that is your choice,' he said. 'I, however, intend to get some sleep.'

He turned on to his side, presenting her this time with an inimical view of his back, as he re-arranged his pillows and extinguished the lamp on his night table.

At first Dana stayed where she was, torn by confusion as she gazed down at the floor, waiting for the blush that had consumed every inch of her skin to subside and her heartbeat to return to something like normality.

But eventually she decided that maintaining her present stance was simply making her look ridiculous, so she reluctantly crossed the room, switched off her own lamp and climbed into bed, lying tensely on her back as far away from Zac as it was possible to get without ending up on the floor, and staring at the ceiling while she waited, with a mixture of longing and dread, for him to reach for her.

But as the minutes passed and began to stretch out into something like eternity, she realised, astonished, that it wasn't going to happen. That his deep, steady breathing was telling her he'd meant what he said about sleeping, and slowly she began to relax, letting herself sink down into the welcoming comfort of the mattress as her flurried anxious breathing steadied.

Realising too that, in a bed this size, it was quite easy to pretend that she was alone.

And that alone was the safest thing to be.

Tomorrow he'll be gone, she thought, suppressing the swift pang twisting sharply inside her. Gone for several weeks, which gives me time to find some way—some strategy to deal with this half-life I've signed up to.

And Zac had done exactly the same, she reminded herself. Maybe he also was regretting his decision. Perhaps this was why he was keeping his distance, so that he didn't turn a mistake into a total disaster.

If—if they didn't have sex, she was almost sure they could get an annulment very quickly, whereas there had to be a statutory period before divorce was permitted.

Maybe the marriage could be quietly ended before its existence became public.

She stirred restlessly, then froze, wary of disturbing him.

Oh, God, what a mess it all was. What a ghastly mess—reaching back to the warm darkness of the summer house all those years ago. To the silent, deceptive magic of his kisses—his touch.

She remembered the friction of his frilled shirt against her bare skin and, lifting her hands to her breasts, she felt the swift hardening of her nipples through the thin fabric that now covered them.

Imagined herself somehow back in that long-ago summer night, but this time unfastening his shirt, fumbling with his waistband and zip as she stripped him in turn. As she touched him everywhere, learning him with her fingertips. Feeling that lithe male body vibrantly, awesomely alive under her seeking hands. His flesh warm under her mouth...

Of course, she'd been too shy, too inexperienced to attempt any such intimacies. And, in so many ways, she hadn't changed. These were still uncharted waters for her.

That night had been like a claw scraping across her senses for seven years, she thought, pressing her clenched fist against her lips. But that had to end now. She could not let herself think about it any more, because if she did, she would be lost.

I won't be able to hide what I feel, she thought. What I want. It's bad enough just being here with him, knowing I would only have to stretch out a hand…

Instead, she put her hand to better use, biting almost savagely at her knuckles. Driving out one pain with another. Except any damage to her skin would heal. The ache inside her could not be so easily assuaged.

Yet how could she willingly surrender herself to a man who'd virtually bought her for sex, and wouldn't care that, with her body, she would give her heart and soul? On the contrary, he was quite cynical enough to find that amusing.

Far better—infinitely safer—to resist the dark temptation he offered and remember that she was fulfilling nothing more than a clause in a contract. Oh, God—nothing more.

She hadn't forgotten Adam's sneering claim that, once a woman belonged to him, Zac became bored and walked away.

And it was hardly likely that a brief legal ceremony would render the future of their marriage any less bleak.

A swift annulment or polite indifference, she thought unhappily. The proverbial rock and the hard place.

Don't go there, she adjured herself almost frantically. If you can't sleep, be practical instead. Think about the rooms that need a transformation. Stand in each of them. Visualise paint, paper and fabrics. Work out a time scale.

Instead she found herself in a long corridor, empty, windowless, its walls and floor painted as white as the ceiling and she began to run towards a door at the far end, desperately searching for colour, for some sign of life, only to have the door slam in her face. And she sank to the floor, closing her eyes against the dazzle of the whiteness.

When she opened them again a moment later, she realised she was not on a wooden floor but in bed, the room bathed in the half-light of early morning.

And made the far more disturbing discovery that somehow in the night she'd moved across the bed to where Zac was lying, and was now held in the curve of his arm, his hand lightly clasping her hip, and her head pillowed on his chest.

How in the world had it happened? she wondered, her throat tightening. But she could worry about that later.

Her immediate need was to extricate herself and move back to the safety zone before Zac woke and jumped to any conclusions.

Biting her lip, she managed, slowly and carefully, to remove his hand from her hip, but as she began to edge away across the bed, Zac stirred, murmuring something unintelligible and, an instant later, he opened his eyes and looked at her, propping himself on an elbow.

There was a tingling pause, then he said softly, *'Buongiorno.'*

Dana stared straight ahead of her. 'I'm sorry. I—I didn't mean to wake you.'

'I believe you,' he said, a note of faint amusement in his voice. 'And there is no need to apologise. I promise you I welcome the disturbance.'

'Yes, of course.' She could hear herself beginning to babble. 'You—you have a plane to catch, and I have a lot to do as well. I probably need to make an early start too.'

He said quite gently, 'That, *mia cara*, is not what I mean, as I think you know.' And, before she could think of an excuse or a protest, he reached out, drawing her gently but inexorably back towards his warm nakedness.

He paused for a long moment, his dark eyes unreadable as he studied her. Then he lifted a hand, stroking back the hair from her flushed, startled face before running a fingertip down the curve of her cheek and brushing her parted lips.

Light as it was, she seemed to feel his touch reaching down into the marrow of her bones. Discovered it echoing in her pulses and lifting the fine hairs on her skin. Felt it stir, deep within her, in an ache of remembered longing.

And with it came fear—not of him, but herself and all that she so desperately needed to keep secret.

From somewhere, she found a voice. 'Please— could we—can't this wait—until after your trip, perhaps? Give me some time to get used to—everything?'

'You don't think, maybe, that seven years is long enough?' The faintly quizzical note in his tone did not deceive her. He was making his intentions clear—telling her that the waiting was over. For good. And for both of them.

He reached out and threw back the covers, making her instantly thankful for the modesty of her nightgown. He, of course, she realised, staring at his chest as if mesmerised, had no such reservations.

And felt herself tense like a coiled spring as she waited for Zac to kiss her—and for all that would inevitably follow.

Closed her eyes, scared of what she might see in his dark face. Triumph, she thought, swallowing. Lust turning to cold determination. Unbearable things.

So she was startled by the gentleness of his mouth as it touched hers, as it moved on the softness of her lips, exploring the delicate contours as if they were the petals of a flower that he did not wish to bruise.

Suddenly the years slipped away and she was seventeen again, her innocent flesh responding in astonished delight to the caresses of her unseen midnight lover.

Now she realised her whole body was reawakening, not just to the shock of sensual pleasure but to the promise of more as one trembling thrill built upon another, winding her in a web of sweetness. Creating a need that threatened to become a necessity as, once again, she lay in the arms of the man she loved…

So much so that her lips were already parting to his insistence, permitting—even welcoming the silken, sensuous provocation of his tongue gliding against her own.

At the same time, his hands were making a slow journey down the entire length of her body, touching her softly, caressingly through the thin material of her nightgown, as if he was committing to memory every curve, every angle, every plane, his fingers returning at last to linger on the swell of her breasts.

He slid the narrow strap of her nightgown from her shoulder, baring one small delicate mound and cupping it in his palm, his thumb teasing the nipple, rousing it to aching pleasure, as his kiss deepened. Beckoned.

But when he pushed down the other strap with the clear intention of uncovering her completely, Dana's faltering reason intervened.

'No—please.' She pushed him away, snatching at the slipping fabric. 'I—I can't…'

'You said you would not resist,' he reminded her quietly.

'Yes—but you don't know what this is like for me. How impossible. I—I'm just not ready.'

Not brave enough to endure. Not strong enough to pretend…

'But will you be any more prepared to surrender in a week—two weeks—a month?' Zac shook his head. 'I doubt it, *mia cara.*'

He paused. 'So, let us make a deal.'

'Another one?' Her voice shook. 'Isn't the first one problem enough?'

'A different one,' he said. 'And perhaps simpler.'

His gaze searched hers. 'If you will try to trust me, *mia bella,*' he whispered, 'I will try to be patient. That is—until you tell me it is no longer necessary. Do you agree?'

For a moment, she was silent, then, knowing how unbearable any alternative might be, and knowing too that it was not him she could not trust, but herself, she gave a small, jerky nod.

There was another, longer pause and she

thought she heard him sigh quietly, then he bent, kissing her forehead and her eyes before his lips found hers again, brushing them gently.

His hand touched her hair, following its silken fall, then moved to the slender curve of her shoulder, smoothing the delicate bone structure and stroking her skin as if he was calming a small, scared animal.

She wanted to resent it, but she couldn't—not when she could feel the tension—the fear—ebbing away—changing under the sheer alchemy of his touch. When, if she was honest, she felt more like nestling closer to him, and purring. While somewhere, deep within her, she felt warm tendrils of excitement growing—spreading.

Zac slid his hands down her arms, spreading them wide, his lips exploring the hollow of an armpit, tracing the blue veins in the bend of her elbow, and the underside of her wrist where her pulse was racing, his fingers linking with hers, holding them as his mouth moved back to her throat, measuring its slender length in a trail of tiny kisses that lighted their own slow fire.

She bit back a little moan as sharp quivers of pleasure lanced through her entire being. Too sharp, she thought, too pleasurable but impossible to evade, even if she wished to do so, when his hands were still clasping hers at her sides, pressing them down into the mattress. Rendering her virtually helpless.

Dana felt herself sinking down into the bed, her breath quickening as his lips continued downwards until they reached the little valley between her breasts where he lingered for an endless moment, his cheek against the scented fullness he had uncovered.

Then, slowly and deliberately, he released her hands, but only so that his own fingers could drift teasingly across her hip bones, her belly, and upwards to her breasts, brushing their creamy swell with his palms while his fingertips, with infinite precision, circled her nipples, already engorged and aching for his touch. An erotic torment he seemed inclined to prolong endlessly.

This time, Dana could not suppress her whimper of longing—of desire as heat flared inside her, fierce and irresistible, forcing her to arch towards him.

'Si, carissima.' His voice was a husky whisper, his words a promise. He paid sensuous homage to the sweetness of her parted lips with the tip of his tongue, then bent to her breasts, cupping them, raising them to his mouth for unhurried adoration before taking one erect rosy peak between his lips and suckling it gently, making her body writhe in delicious agony as each stroke of his tongue sent the tide of arousal surging through her entire being.

He slid a hand down the length of her body, his warm tantalising fingers reaching under the rucked-up hem of her nightgown to caress her thigh, so desperately near to the hot, moist centre of her where she craved him, but not near enough.

Her body was in ferment with the frustration of pleasure withheld, melting, scalding with the need to know and be known. A harsh sob rising in her throat, she took his hand and carried it to the joining of her thighs as they slackened and parted to receive him for the first intimate exploration her body had ever experienced.

His touch was light but exquisitely, terrifyingly precise, gliding between the delicate folds of woman flesh to find the tiny sensitive nub they protected and caressing it slowly and rhythmically, coaxing it to become erect under the subtle, enticing play of his fingers. Dana heard her breathing change as her entire conscious being seemed to turn inward upon itself, concentrating blindly on sensations she had not realised could exist or that her starved body would ever feel.

Zac's hand moved fractionally, traversing the slick wetness he'd created to allow his fingers to reach and gently penetrate the entrance to her vagina, pushing into her, then withdrawing. Inciting, then withholding. While, all the time, the ball of his thumb was continuing, intensifying its erotic stimulation of her tiny, swollen bud.

Gasping, Dana became aware of an odd stirring deep inside her as if a coiled spring was tightening endlessly.

She felt as if she was tottering on the edge of an abyss. That her entire inner self was gathering, preparing itself in some impossible way for a leap into the unknown.

She wanted to scream at him to stop because she couldn't bear it—knowing that if he did stop she would die…

And at that moment the abyss took her and, as she fell, she felt her body implode into the first throbbing, rapturous convulsions of release. Heard herself cry out as the pleasure reached an almost agonised crescendo, then found herself drifting, sighing and weightless, back to earth.

Where she found Zac watching her, propped on one elbow, his faint smile tender rather than triumphant, and reflective—even, she thought out of her own welter of emotional confusion, tinged with something like regret.

He said softly, *'Carissima,'* and she looked back at him, eyes widening as she absorbed every bronze inch of him, finally allowing her gaze to linger on the powerful, rigid shaft springing up from his loins. Aware, to her own astonishment, that her womanhood was already tightening in what could only be anticipation, and renewed desire.

Telling her that the delight he'd given her was only a beginning.

As, she told herself, she would now demonstrate…

She sat up, holding his gaze, and slowly pulled her crumpled nightgown over her head, tossing it aside, before lying back naked, her whole body an invitation under the sudden flare of his dark eyes.

She saw a muscle move in his throat, then he came to join her, kneeling between her legs as he bent to kiss her, and she reached up to caress his shoulders and upper arms, feeling his hard muscles clench at her touch.

His mouth took hers without haste, his hands slow and careful as they travelled over her, outlining her slenderness almost as if he was learning her by heart, adoring her breasts as they lifted eagerly to his lips, outlining the hollows of her pelvis, skimming the concavity of her belly, running his fingertips down the slim length of her legs.

And she touched him too, her hands sweeping down the length of his back to the firm buttocks, revelling in this newfound freedom. Watching the heat burn along his cheekbones and hearing the harsh rasp of his breathing when her fingers at last closed round the hardness of him, sliding from the base to the moist tip. Glorying in his soft groan of pleasure as the stroke of her hand became more daring. And more demanding.

And when he positioned himself over her, she spread herself beneath him.

Telling him without words that she was ready and so much more than willing.

Yet his possession of her was as unhurried as his previous caresses, giving an impression of passion firmly controlled as he eased his way into her pliant body, watching her face for any sign of discomfort.

But if there was pain it was fleeting, and anyway overwhelmed by the need to have Zac sheathing himself in her, filling her with total completion. Making her his woman at last.

For a moment he remained still, looking down into her unclouded eyes, then he began to move inside her, and she lifted her hands to clasp his shoulders, rising and falling with him as she echoed each long, slow thrust, taking him ever more deeply into her, tightening around him as her body quickened to every new and powerful sensation that he was evoking.

In answer, Zac began to move faster, even urgently as if some culmination was approaching, and Dana, gasping, felt once again that first elusive curl of exquisite tension twist inside her, driving her on too, forcing her to reach for it, her breath sobbing almost in desperation.

Only for Zac's hand to slip down between their joined bodies to find her tiny erect pinnacle, and stroke it. And, even as he touched her, she was lost, crying out in ecstasy as her body splintered into wild pulsating abandonment.

Hearing him call her name, his voice hoarse and anguished, and feeling deep within her the spurting heat of his own climax.

CHAPTER THIRTEEN

AFTERWARDS THERE WAS SILENCE. Zac lifted himself away from her and turned on his back, an arm flung across his eyes as he fought to control his breathing.

Dana remained still. She knew it must still be early but even so the room seemed to be bathed in sunlight. She felt totally boneless—too languid even to lift a finger, but at the same time suffused with wellbeing. Her skin was tingling as if every pore was charged with some magical form of electricity.

She turned her head slowly and looked at Zac. She wanted to say something—express how she felt—how he had made her feel during this entire glorious initiation—but she was lost for words.

'Thank you' seemed inappropriate, even ludicrous, while 'I love you' was out of the question.

Besides, she was hoping he would be the one to speak.

Eventually, she reached out and touched his sweat-dampened shoulder. 'Zac? Shouldn't we—talk?'

Oh, God, she thought. That sounded such a cliché at what should be a pivotal moment in their lives.

He didn't reply immediately and she wondered if he was asleep. Then: 'Later,' he said. 'Now we both need to rest. We both have a busy day ahead of us.'

It was not the response she'd hoped for but she wasn't going to argue. She waited, wondering if he would take her in his arms, hoping that he might, but he simply turned on his side away from her, and after a disappointed pause, Dana did the same.

I can wait, she told herself. Until later.

And burrowing her cheek into her pillow, she smiled.

She'd not really expected to sleep. After all, she had too much to think about, too much to plan, yet eventually she did.

And awoke with a start, wondering what had disturbed her.

It was certainly not Zac, because she was alone

in the big bed. And that surprise was followed by another when she discovered she was once again wearing her nightdress which, presumably, he had replaced at some point.

My God, she thought, stretching. I must have been dead to the world.

And then she heard the discreet tap on the door and Mrs Harris's voice saying, 'Your tea, madam,' and realised what had woken her, a glance at the bedside clock informing her it was nearly 10:00 a.m.

She sat up quickly, straightening the covers and called an embarrassed, 'Come in.'

Mrs Harris also seemed flustered as she placed the folding tray across Dana's lap and went to draw the curtains, filling the room with sunshine.

A beautiful day, thought Dana, just as she'd expected. However, one glance showed her that the little white porcelain teapot, the cup, saucer and milk jug were intended for single use.

'Is my—my husband having coffee?' she asked.

'Mr Belisandro breakfasted some time ago, madam.' She added with slight constraint, 'His driver and one of the gardeners are taking his luggage down to the car.'

'Already?' Alarmed, Dana lifted the tray aside and threw back the covers. 'But I need to talk to him.'

Tell him that he'll have to take a later flight because I'm going to Europe with him, even if it is a working honeymoon.

That, she thought, had been her last conscious resolve before sleep claimed her and it was still the plan.

Barefoot, she flew across to his dressing room only to find it deserted, the closet doors standing wide, the drawers left open, revealing emptiness.

Good God, she thought helplessly. He's taking everything. No wonder he needed two of them to carry it all.

She turned back to the housekeeper. 'Can you get my robe and slippers, please? Is Mr Belisandro still in the dining room?'

The older woman hesitated awkwardly. 'I believe he's occupied in the book room, madam.'

Tying the sash of her white satin robe, Dana hurried downstairs. The front door was open, and she could see the chauffeur loading suitcases into the boot of the car.

What the hell is going on? she asked herself, as she reached the book room and marched in.

Zac was standing at the surprisingly bare desk, checking the contents of his briefcase. At her entry, he glanced up, his mouth tightening.

Dana closed the door behind her and leaned against it, trying to hide the fact that she'd begun to feel oddly nervous.

'You said we'd talk, she reminded him quietly. 'This seems more like the last minute than later.'

'I decided it would be best.' He picked up a large manila envelope and held it out to her. 'I have a wedding gift for you.'

Dana remained where she was, fighting a strange compulsion to put her hands behind her back and keep them there.

'Thank you,' she said. 'I think. What is it, please?'

'The deeds of this house,' he said. 'Transferred into your sole name, with a letter to tell you that Mannion now belongs to you alone.' He paused. 'So, at last we both possess what we most desired and our bargain is completed, leaving us free to get on with our separate lives.'

'Separate,' Dana repeated. The room was

warm but she suddenly felt very cold. 'I don't understand.'

'Yet it is not difficult. You wanted this house. I wanted you.' He shrugged. 'The deal is done—certainly to my satisfaction and I hope to yours also,' he added, glancing down at the envelope. 'This travesty of a marriage has fulfilled its purpose and there is no need for us to continue with it any further. When my European trip is ended, I shall find other accommodation.' His smile did not reach his eyes. 'I am sure you will find this a relief.'

She was glad of the door's support, or she might have collapsed on to the floor.

Her voice barely above a whisper, she said, 'You mean you're—not coming back?' She tried to think of some convincing reason for her concern. 'But what about all the work being done on the house?'

'You need no one else to make your dream for Mannion come true,' he said after a pause. 'And there are funds available for that, as I made clear last night.'

'But surely you want to see how it turns out. How your money has been spent.'

'No,' he said. 'It is of no great interest to me. This is your dream, *cara mia*, not mine.' He paused again. 'I have also made provision for your personal maintenance. If you find it inadequate in any way, please contact my lawyers.'

'But you can't just go.' She tried to sound reasonable—rational when she was screaming inside. 'What will people think?'

'It will be assumed we married in haste, and our repentance was almost instantaneous,' he said, his mouth curling. 'Besides, we have both had what we wanted, so the opinions of others do not matter.'

'But—Nicola's wedding...'

'Naturally, I shall return for that. But you need not fear,' he added with swift harshness as her eyes flew to his face. 'My stay will be brief, and I shall use the single bed in the dressing room.'

She said huskily, 'Then last night meant—nothing...'

'On the contrary,' Zac drawled. 'What do you want me to say, *mia bella*? That you were enchanting—a ravishing delight as you fulfilled our agreement? I admit it. I had not expected such generosity from you. Particularly when it was to be our first and last time together.'

'No,' she said in a voice she did not recognise. 'But then I could hardly expect that either.' It was her turn to pause. 'And the legal end to our—deal. Divorce. When will that take place?'

'As soon as it can be arranged, although it is unlikely to be immediate. There are rules to be followed.'

'Yes,' she said, dry-mouthed. 'I'm sure there are.' She stood away from the door, lifting her chin. 'Well—there seems little more to be said.'

Except that wasn't true. There was so very much more—like begging 'Don't leave me. Don't go. Take me with you' as she clung to him.

Except he might still walk away, and she would simply have set herself up for more misery. More humiliation.

'No,' he agreed. 'It seems not.' He fastened his briefcase. 'Then—*addio*, Dana *mia*. Allow me to hope that Mannion proves to be everything you have hoped for over so many long years.'

He put the envelope with the deeds on the desk, and with a swift, impersonal smile walked past her into the hall.

Moments later, she heard the car start and drive away.

And Dana stood, her arms wrapped round her body, listening with bleak intensity until the last note of the engine had died away and she knew that he was gone.

Work was the thing. That was what she told herself before she tried to sleep each night and when she woke exhausted in the morning. Work would get her through this nightmare. Because, with an army of painters and decorators in the house, there was little opportunity to give way to her feelings.

To crawl into some dark place and weep until there were no tears left.

Instead, she had to liaise with Bella Dixon, the designer who'd created the bedroom Dana could now hardly bear to look at, discussing colour schemes, fabrics and patterns for the rest of the house.

My dream come true, just like Zac said, she thought with irony, and I'm living with it. Dying with it by inches as I watch it all taking shape, like an observer admiring the work without elation or any sense of possession.

At the same time, she had to keep up a front with Nicola, who was growing happier and more excited all the time as the big day approached.

And, which was far worse, fending off her questions about how Zac's European trip was going and when he'd be returning.

Throughout that entire first day, she'd lived in a kind of suspended disbelief, waiting and hoping that by some miracle he would change his mind and return.

And even though she'd eventually and painfully forced herself to accept that Adam's cruel and jeering warning had been no more than the truth and that, having had her, Zac was no longer interested in even a repeat performance, let alone any real relationship, she'd anticipated at least some contact, however minimal—a phone call—a text—an email in the endless, agonising days that followed.

And how could she confide in Nicola—or anyone? Confess how—or why—her marriage had so suddenly become this overwhelming disaster.

From the start she'd blamed Zac for having her sent away seven years earlier, and yet hadn't she too been at fault in trying to further her aims by that foolish, headlong pursuit of Adam? And, knowing Adam as he clearly did, perhaps Zac'd had good reason to think she and Mannion were better apart.

But it had given her an excuse ever since to regard her ongoing preoccupation with Zac as dislike and resentment, closing her eyes and her heart to any other possibility. Telling herself her shock at seeing him again was born from anger, not desire. Focusing with icy determination on claiming her right to Mannion by whatever means became necessary, 'Be careful what you wish for' had been one of Aunt Joss's admonishments. 'Because you might get it.'

But I ignored that, she acknowledged with a pang. Just as I wouldn't listen to Zac's warning about greed. And now the substance of my life has gone for ever, and I'm left with the shadow.

And I'm even fooling myself about that. Because Zac was never going to be mine to have and to hold, along with all the other promises in the Marriage Service. And maybe I should be thankful that he never realised how I truly felt. Because that would have left me with even more shame—more trauma to contend with when he walked out.

Is there a guardian angel for idiots too blind and stupid to understand their own hearts? Surely there must be.

Yet, she thought, maybe there was something to be salvaged from the wreckage. A way to justify what she'd done and the decisions she'd made.

When the wedding was over, she could heal the scars of her mother's rejection by the Latimers and end her exile in Spain by offering her the permanent home she should always have had— at Mannion.

And maybe she could herself find comfort in building this new relationship with a woman she hardly knew. Take satisfaction in someone else's dream coming true at last.

She sat down that evening and wrote a letter to Linda, filling her invitation with warmth and encouragement and even a shy attempt at affection.

Telling herself that surely her mother would respond this time. Making a silent promise that, if not, she would go to Spain to this—Roberto's Bar and persuade her face to face to accompany her back to England.

And that she would totally refuse to take no for an answer.

Some good has to emerge from all this, she thought. It must. Because it's all I have left to believe in.

CHAPTER FOURTEEN

THERE WAS A feeling of autumn in the air, Dana thought ruefully as she drove down the hill towards Mannion. Or was it just her imagination telling her that she had nothing ahead of her but a long, cold winter?

On the other hand the cooler, showery weather of the past week was supposed to revert to sunshine again in time for the wedding.

Her visits to the caterers and the florist in the nearby town had reassured her that everything was proceeding as planned, as she would tell Nicola, who was beginning to show signs of bridal nerves.

Dana was nervous too, shaking inside at the prospect of seeing Zac again, and sick at heart at the pretence of married bliss she would have to keep up until the wedding was over and everyone was gone.

Everyone, she repeated silently, her throat tightening.

But she couldn't allow herself to think like that. Instead, she had to concentrate on practicalities.

Like telling Nic that her cake is beautiful, she thought, and that the Vicar's wife is personally supervising the white and gold floral decorations in the church in case old Mrs Wilmot tries to smother the pews in pink spray carnations.

At Mannion, the decorators were putting the finishing touches to the bedroom Aunt Joss would occupy, bringing that part of the refurbishment to an end.

Dana's feelings about seeing Miss Grantham again were still mixed. She wished so much that she was the kind of aunt who'd encourage her to sob out her bewilderment and heartbreak in her lap, instead of treating her with the chilly disapproval which was the more likely reaction.

Nor had she heard a word from Linda—not even an acknowledgement of her letter—so a trip to Spain might be on the cards after all.

And maybe a break would do her good. She still wasn't sleeping well, her dreams filled with great empty houses where she wandered from one deserted room to another, searching—always searching, yet finding nothing.

As she reached the house, she saw a strange car was parked on the other side of the main entrance and, for a moment, her heart leapt in swift painful hope, until common sense reminded her that Zac's car was different from this other one in size, colour, make and probably every other respect.

Mrs Harris was waiting for her in the hall. 'There's a visitor for you, madam. A Mr Harvey and quite insistent about seeing you. I've put him in the drawing room.'

'Harvey?' Dana repeated slowly. 'That's vaguely familiar.'

Mrs Harris looked austere. 'He seems a bit rough and ready to me.'

Dana smiled at her. 'Well, let's smooth the edges with some coffee, please, Janet.'

Mr Harvey, rising politely to his feet at Dana's entrance, was a stockily built man, middle-aged, bald and deeply tanned, with a round cheerful face, currently unsmiling. He was wearing well-cut grey slacks, a florid shirt, and an expensive-looking linen jacket.

He said, 'So you're Dana.'

'Yes,' she agreed coolly. 'And you are…?'

'I'm Bob Harvey,' he said. 'Your stepfather.'

'Stepfather,' Dana echoed, feeling dazed. 'I don't understand.'

'It's simple enough,' he said. 'Your mother and I got married eight months ago. I knew her from years back when she worked for me at the Royal Oak, and I couldn't believe my eyes when I walked into this bar I was thinking of buying in Altamejo, and found her there serving the drinks. It was the best thing that's happened to me in years.'

'I—I see.' Dana sat down on the opposite sofa. 'Well, congratulations. I hope you'll be very happy.'

'We're getting there,' he said. 'But it would be easier if you'd stop writing to her about—all this.' He waved a disparaging hand at his surroundings.

'I'm sure you mean well,' he went on. 'But your letters just remind Linda of things best forgotten, and do her no good at all, so I want them to stop.'

Dana sat up very straight. 'Mr Harvey,' she said, 'I also have my mother's best interests at heart. And I want her to know that she is welcome to come back to Mannion and take the rightful place she's always been denied.'

'Well, that's where you're wrong, love,' he said. 'Because *rightful* doesn't enter into it. That's been the trouble all along.'

There was a tap at the door and Janet Harris came in with a tray of coffee and homemade biscuits, forcing Dana to dam back her flood of angry questions.

'You think Jack Latimer was your father,' Mr Harvey said as soon as the housekeeper had gone. 'But he wasn't. Linda lied about it—and to people who mattered and who knew better. And then, like a damned fool, she went on lying until there was no way back from the disgrace she'd made for herself.'

Dana set the coffee pot down with a bang. 'How dare you say these things? I was with my mother. I saw the terrible effect that Mrs Latimer's rejection had on her. How she grieved for my father.'

He looked at her squarely. 'And I suppose you think I'm lying too.' He shook his head. 'Not so. Because I'm the only person on earth who does know the truth, which I heard from my Linda's own lips before we were married.'

'But why should she have lied?' Dana demanded.

'Do you have to ask?' Another derisive wave of the hand. 'Just look round you. She wanted all this. She wanted to be someone, instead of a struggling single mother, and Jack Latimer was her chance at the good life' He paused. 'And because he was no longer around to argue, poor lad, she took it.'

Dana sat for a long moment with her face in her hands.

Eventually she said huskily, 'You mean there was never a relationship between them?'

'Oh, there was that,' he said soberly. 'For a while. Just—no baby. He couldn't, you see. He'd caught mumps just at the wrong time, and it had made him sterile. His family knew it, but Linda didn't.'

'But she was so sure. So bitter about the way she'd been treated.'

'So guilty about what she'd done,' he said.

'You don't know what it was like to be there—to live with it.'

'No,' he said. 'And she's still ashamed of what it did to you. Too ashamed to face you yet as well.

But it will happen—maybe when she finds she's going to be a grandmother.'

For a stricken moment, Dana felt what it must have been like to be Linda. To have made such a terrible mistake and realise there was no way back. To have to live with her punishment…

She said quietly, hopelessly, 'But I believed all she ever wanted was Mannion.'

'So did she,' he said. He smiled suddenly. 'But she knows better now. And so do you, my dear, being a newlywed yourself.'

He got to his feet. 'Just give her a bit more time, and everything will work out for the best. You'll see.'

He looked at his watch. 'And I must be on my way. My sister's expecting me.'

Dana rose too. 'Mr Harvey—I have to know. Is it—are you my father?'

He sighed. 'I wish I could say yes, but it would be just another lie. It's one thing your mother hasn't told me but perhaps, one day, she'll tell you.'

He added quietly, 'And you mustn't worry about her, love. I'll make sure she's all right. And I'll see myself out.'

Alone, Dana sat, staring into space, her mind whirling until Janet Harris arrived to remove the tray. 'But you haven't touched your coffee,' she exclaimed.

Dana looked up, a small bleak smile twisting her lips. 'No,' she said. 'We didn't. Do you know, Janet, I think I'm going to have a very large whisky instead.'

'It's just beautiful,' Nicola said wistfully. 'Exactly like Mannion should be again. Bringing back all sorts of happy memories as well.' She sighed, then perked up. 'And I can't believe how much you've done in the time.'

Dana smiled, at the same time giving her a thoughtful glance. 'Thank Bella Dixon and her troops, not me. And not everyone's so admiring,' she added wryly. 'Your Aunt Mimi took one look at her room and said all that cream made her feel as if she'd be sleeping in a dairy.'

Nicola pulled a face. 'Aunt Mimi will never change. She's already told my father that Mannion would have been his if he'd only stayed in England, and that Zac drove Adam out.'

Dana gasped. 'What did he say?'

'He didn't,' Nicola returned with faint grimness. 'The terrible Sadie cut in and informed her that it was none of her damned business, and for all the use Adam was in Australia, Mannion could have him back and welcome.'

For the first time in several days, Dana laughed out loud. 'Good for Sadie,' she said. 'She's my type of woman.'

'I'll gift-wrap her for you,' said Nicola. She paused. 'Is everything all right? I thought you'd be bouncing off the walls at the prospect of being with Zac again. Regarding which,' she went on cheerfully. 'If the pair of you want to snatch a couple of hours alone together for a real reunion, I'll make sure you're not disturbed.'

Dana's face warmed. 'What and give Aunt Mimi more ammunition?' she said with forced lightness. 'No, I intend to be the perfect hostess.'

Adding silently, *For the first and last time.*

She had time to practise her role. There was still an hour or more before Zac would arrive, according to the message he'd left with Janet, bringing Serafina and Aunt Joss with him.

Time to ensure she'd be able to greet him with

calm composure and conduct their subsequent business meeting in the same way.

She'd dressed carefully too, choosing a slim-fitting knee-length linen dress, the colour of a briar rose, which gave a tinge of warmth to her pallor.

And chatting to the Marchwoods, who told her how pretty she looked, helped, of course, reminding Dana how blessed Nicola was in her in-laws.

But being cornered by Jo and Emily, both bursting with curiosity about her hasty marriage, was very different and far more difficult.

'You're a slyboots,' Emily teased. 'I didn't think you and the gorgeous Mr Belisandro were even remotely involved. In fact, I thought...' She checked. 'Well, that doesn't matter. So, tell all. How did you get together?'

'I've known him nearly all my life,' said Dana.

Except I didn't truly know him, she thought. Or myself. And now it's too late.

When Janet told her the car was coming up the drive, she hung back, making sure that Nicola and Eddie were heading the welcome party, telling herself they were the ones Serafina would want to see. And that her self-effacement was not because her mouth was dry and her stomach churning in a maelstrom of excitement and panic as she realised that, at any moment, she would see Zac again, even if it was only for another twenty-four hours.

Serafina was the first to enter the house, still upright in spite of her stick, her silver hair arranged in the same elegant coronet, her face lighting up with the old charm when she saw Nicola.

At least I got that right, thought Dana, as she received an unsmiling nod from Aunt Joss, who was following close behind.

She swallowed, her hands clenching into fists at her sides, her eyes fixed almost painfully on the sunlit doorway as she waited for Zac.

Her first thought was that he looked bone-weary, his dark eyes brooding as if his body might be here but his thoughts were miles away.

Darling, she thought. Oh, my darling.

And, conquering the impulse to run to him, to hold him close and pour out her heart, she walked slowly forward, wearing a smile that might have been nailed there.

'Dana *mia*.' He kissed her hand and then her cheek, his lips barely brushing her skin.

'Welcome home.' She kept smiling. 'Did you have a good trip?'

'A successful one.' He took her hand and led her over to Serafina. 'May I present your new cousin, *cara mia*?'

'She is hardly a stranger,' the older woman said drily, shaking hands briefly and formally. 'We will talk later, no doubt, but the journey has tired me a little and I would like to go to my room.'

'Of course.' Dana hesitated. 'Perhaps you would also prefer to have tea upstairs rather than in the drawing room. Lapsang Souchong, isn't it?'

'Why, yes,' Mrs Latimer acknowledged with faint surprise. 'You have a good memory.'

As Dana watched Janet escort the two women upstairs, Zac said quietly, 'I would prefer coffee in the book room, if you please. I have some work—a few loose ends from the trip—to complete. Perhaps you will excuse me to our guests and say I will see them at dinner.'

A heading under which she was presumably included, thought Dana, turning away.

When everyone had been served with the food and drink of their choice in the preferred location, she slipped away upstairs and knocked on her aunt's door.

'So you won in the end' was Miss Grantham's uncompromising welcome. 'I suppose I should congratulate you, although I thought Mr Belisandro would have had more sense.'

'Because he got me sent away seven years ago?' Dana queried tautly. 'I suppose everyone's entitled to second thoughts.' However short-lived...

Aunt Joss stared at her. 'What on earth are you talking about?'

'My terrible teenage faux pas.' Dana lifted her chin. 'The disgraceful pass he alleged I made at him.'

'But that wasn't Zac.' Her aunt frowned. 'The complaint came from Mr Adam.' She shook her head. 'Not that it matters. It was a long time ago.'

'Yes,' Dana said dazedly. 'A very long time ago.' And every day of it, she thought, I've blamed Zac for something he didn't do.

She took a long, shaky breath. 'But I'm not actually here for that. Did you know my mother was married?'

It was Aunt Joss's turn to look pole-axed.

'Married? To whom, for heaven's sake? Some Spaniard?'

'To Bob Harvey, her former boss at the Royal Oak,' Dana returned levelly. 'Accordingly, I now know that Jack Latimer could never have been my father and why, and that neither Linda nor I have ever had any legal right to any part of the Mannion estate. That it's always been a bag of moonshine.'

'Linda admitted that?'

'Only to her husband. Perhaps you could tell Mrs Latimer on my behalf, and assure her that I intend to—adjust the situation.' She paused. 'I— we'll talk again later—if you want.'

The door to the book room was closed, and Zac's voice was impatient when he called *'Entrare'* in reply to her knock.

His expression as he looked at her across the paper-strewn desk was not encouraging. 'Dana— unless this is important...'

'Yes,' she said. 'It is. Very important.'

His eyes narrowed, then he put down his pen and rose slowly. He came round the desk, leaning back against it as if he was bracing himself.

He said quietly, 'Have you come to tell me that you may be expecting our child?'

Child...

She repeated the word silently, every inch of her suddenly burning as anguish twisted inside her. Asking herself what would happen if she was to tell a lie. If she pretended there was a baby coming from that solitary night in his arms. Telling herself with a kind of desperation that, if it persuaded him to stay with her, she would make it the truth.

If...

Because there was no guarantee that he would do any such thing. That he might simply promise child support—and still walk away.

I'd be no better than my mother, she thought. A gambler who lost everything. And worse.

She clenched her hands at her sides to hide the fact that they were trembling. 'No, it—it isn't that.'

Face expressionless, Zac looked down at the floor. 'I see. What then?'

She swallowed. 'It's about the house.'

'*Santa Madonna.*' The words seemed ground out of him. '*Sì, naturalmente.* It would have to be the house. What else has it ever been? You need more money? Take it. You wish to pull it down and begin again? Do so. It is no longer my concern. Only yours. Or did I fail to make that clear?'

'It's nothing like that,' she said. 'I came to say that I want to sell it.'

'To sell—Mannion?' There was an odd note in his voice.

'Yes,' she returned baldly, adding, 'I—I thought you would wish to know.'

'Why? Do you want my advice? I am sure your former employers are better placed to assist you. Or do you need me to recommend a lawyer, perhaps?' He shrugged. 'Contact our legal department. Any of them will be glad to help.'

'Yes,' she said. 'I'm sure they would.' Glad to help rid you of your unwanted encumbrances. To set you free again.

She could feel misery knotting in her chest. Tears threatening that she could not—would not allow to fall.

She said huskily, 'I can make my own arrangements, thank you. I've said all I came to say and please forgive me for interrupting you.'

As she turned to leave, Zac said abruptly, '*Un momento*. Wait.'

'Are you worried I'll sell at a loss?' She shook her head. 'I won't.'

'I wish to know why you are selling at all.'

'Because I no longer wish to live here.'

'After all these years when you thought of nothing else—wanted nothing else?' he asked harshly. 'I cannot accept that.'

'I've always believed that if Jack Latimer hadn't been killed, he'd have married my mother and, as his daughter, I'd have had a legal right to his estate. I now know that isn't true. That even if he did have an affair with my mother, there could never have been a child because of the illness he suffered in adolescence. That my mother's entire story was a tissue of lies.' She shrugged. 'And I can't live with that.'

'You do not have to,' he said swiftly. 'Mannion has come to you as my gift to my wife.'

'Wife!' She almost choked on the word. 'And how much longer will I continue to be your wife? And when it's over, how many years will I have to spend here without you—in Serafina's empty shell?'

Her laugh was a sob. 'Surviving in this heap of stones in the middle of nowhere, wandering from room to room, pretending that being alone is just a bad dream, and that somewhere I'll find you waiting for me.'

She flung back her head. 'Well, no, thanks. I can't stay here. There are just too many memories and I won't be able to bear them, so I'll cut my losses right now, if it's all the same to you.'

Her voice broke and she turned, fumbling for the door handle, and heard him say, in little more than a whisper, 'Dana, my love, my wife, *mi adorata*—don't leave me. Don't go.'

The words she had said in her heart so many times.

She looked back and saw his face, as never before, pleading, vulnerable, haggard with yearning and something close to despair.

Caught between hope and uncertainty, she heard herself ask, 'Do you want me?'

'More than that,' he said unsteadily. 'I love you. I think I have loved you always—for the whole of my life, even before I met you. But, until this moment, I thought you only cared for this house. And that is why I went away because I too found I could not bear it.'

With a little cry, she went to him. Went into his arms, yielding her mouth to the storm of his kisses and her body to the fever of his shaking hands. Seeing him for the first time, starving, driven and completely out of control. Glorying in his urgency, as he lifted her on to the desk, sweeping the papers to the floor.

He pushed up her dress, tearing aside her briefs and dragging down his zip, entering her without any preliminaries except their mutual, frantic need of each other. Thrusting into her with passionate, agonised intensity as she clung to him, her body clenching round him, meeting his fire with her own until they were both consumed, gasping their joy into each other's mouths as they rose together to the exquisite savagery of release.

Time steadied. Sanity returned, bringing with it laughter, tenderness and a breathless wonder that they had found each other at last.

Their clothing restored to a more decorous level, they shared the armchair by the fireplace, Dana curled up on her husband's lap, her face buried in his neck while he whispered softly to her in his own language.

'I must learn to speak Italian,' she murmured. 'So that I can understand what you're saying.'

He gave her a lazy grin. 'Tonight, in bed, *mia carissima*, I promise that you shall have a full translation.'

'Mmm.' She nestled closer. 'I can hardly wait.' She sighed. 'But it's a shame you had the summer house pulled down. It would have been nice to go back there before we leave.'

'You still wish to sell Mannion? Even though it brought us together?'

'It could just as easily have driven us apart,' Dana said soberly. 'And it will always remind me of how blind I was.' She shuddered. 'How greedy. How mercenary.'

'No, my darling.' He silenced her gently, a finger on her lips. 'Never that. Only confused and very unhappy. Your mother did her work too well.'

He added, 'And it was Adam who destroyed the summer house. His final act of spite before he handed Mannion to me.'

She said in a low voice, 'I always thought it was you who had me sent away—after that night. But that was Adam, too.'

'He could never forgive a slight,' Zac said after

a pause. 'And I suspect he knew that we were there together when he came looking for you.'

'But why didn't you tell Serafina the truth?'

'Because I was ashamed of myself. I had not intended matters to go as far as they did, but you were so sweet, *mia cara*. So utterly irresistible. But, at the same time, too young for the serious commitment I already knew that I wanted.

'Also,' he added drily, 'I seemed to be the last man in the world you would ever consider as a husband. So, I let you go—told myself to forget you. Except—I could not. But when I saw you again, I realised nothing had changed. That you were still obsessed with Mannion. And that I wanted you more than life itself. So I decided to make both our wishes come true. I told myself that once you were my wife, I could teach you to love me.'

'Then why did you leave?' She flushed a little. 'You must have known how you'd made me feel.'

'Yes,' he said. 'But I also knew that giving you pleasure in bed was not enough. That, in fact, I was the greedy one because I wanted more than your body, my sweet one. I wanted your heart and soul as well, and nothing less would do.'

'And now you have me,' she said. 'All of me. Wherever you are master, I shall be mistress. For ever.'

'*Mi adorata,*' he said softly and kissed her.

* * * * *

If you loved Sara Craven's take on the SEVEN SEXY SINS, *you won't want to miss the rest of this sizzling series!*

Cathy Williams – Sloth –
TO SIN WITH THE TYCOON

Dani Collins – Lust –
THE SHEIKH'S SINFUL SEDUCTION

Kim Lawrence – Pride –
THE SINS OF SEBASTIAN REY-DEFOE

Maggie Cox – Gluttony –
A TASTE OF SIN

Annie West – Envy –
THE SINNER'S MARRIAGE REDEMPTION

Maya Blake – Wrath –
A MARRIAGE FIT FOR A SINNER

Sara Craven – Greed –
THE INNOCENT'S SINFUL CRAVING

MILLS & BOON®
Large Print – April 2016

The Price of His Redemption
Carol Marinelli

Back in the Brazilian's Bed
Susan Stephens

The Innocent's Sinful Craving
Sara Craven

Brunetti's Secret Son
Maya Blake

Talos Claims His Virgin
Michelle Smart

Destined for the Desert King
Kate Walker

Ravensdale's Defiant Captive
Melanie Milburne

The Best Man & The Wedding Planner
Teresa Carpenter

Proposal at the Winter Ball
Jessica Gilmore

Bodyguard...to Bridegroom?
Nikki Logan

Christmas Kisses with Her Boss
Nina Milne

MILLS & BOON®
Large Print – May 2016

The Queen's New Year Secret
Maisey Yates

Wearing the De Angelis Ring
Cathy Williams

The Cost of the Forbidden
Carol Marinelli

Mistress of His Revenge
Chantelle Shaw

Theseus Discovers His Heir
Michelle Smart

The Marriage He Must Keep
Dani Collins

Awakening the Ravensdale Heiress
Melanie Milburne

His Princess of Convenience
Rebecca Winters

Holiday with the Millionaire
Scarlet Wilson

The Husband She'd Never Met
Barbara Hannay

Unlocking Her Boss's Heart
Christy McKellen

MILLS & BOON®

Why shop at millsandboon.co.uk?

Each year, thousands of romance readers find their perfect read at millsandboon.co.uk. That's because we're passionate about bringing you the very best romantic fiction. Here are some of the advantages of shopping at www.millsandboon.co.uk:

* **Get new books first**—you'll be able to buy your favourite books one month before they hit the shops

* **Get exclusive discounts**—you'll also be able to buy our specially created monthly collections, with up to 50% off the RRP

* **Find your favourite authors**—latest news, interviews and new releases for all your favourite authors and series on our website, plus ideas for what to try next

* **Join in**—once you've bought your favourite books, don't forget to register with us to rate, review and join in the discussions

Visit **www.millsandboon.co.uk**
for all this and more today!